DEVINE

Pinkerton detective Nimrod Dunn is hired by Lieutenant Governor Maddox Kingsley to infiltrate an outlaw gang. But when Nimrod's cover is blown, an innocent life is lost in the raging gun battle. The fearsome US Marshal Jake T. Devine then sets about bringing the outlaw Cornelius to justice — but his methods are as brutal as those whom he pursues. With Devine's blood-soaked trail making a mockery of the governor's promise to clean up the county, Maddox must call on Nimrod's services once more — to kill Marshal Devine . . .

Books by I. J. Parnham in the Linford Western Library:

THE OUTLAWED DEPUTY
THE LAST RIDER FROM HELL
BAD DAY IN DIRTWOOD
DEVINE'S LAW
YATES'S DILEMMA
DEAD BY SUNDOWN
CALHOUN'S BOUNTY
CALLOWAY'S CROSSING
BAD MOON OVER DEVIL'S RIDGE
MASSACRE AT BLUFF POINT
THE GALLOWS GANG
RIDERS OF THE BARREN PLAINS
SHARPSHOOTER McCLURE
RAILROAD TO REDEMPTION
BLEACHED BONES IN THE DUST
THE SECRET OF DEVIL'S CANYON
THE PRAIRIE MAN
SHERIFF WITHOUT A STAR
THE SEARCH FOR THE LONE STAR
BEYOND REDEMPTION

I. J. PARNHAM

DEVINE

Complete and Unabridged

LINFORD
Leicester

First published in Great Britain in 2012 by
Robert Hale Limited
London

First Linford Edition
published 2014
by arrangement with
Robert Hale Limited
London

*A catalogue record for this book is available
from the British Library.*

ISBN 978–1–4448–2104–8

Published by
F. A. Thorpe (Publishing)
Anstey, Leicestershire

Set by Words & Graphics Ltd.
Anstey, Leicestershire
Printed and bound in Great Britain by
T. J. International Ltd., Padstow, Cornwall

This book is printed on acid-free paper

1

'One of you,' Cornelius Lee said, 'isn't the man he claims to be.'

Nimrod Dunn's only reaction was to cast suspicious glares at the other men in the room. He was relieved that he didn't receive any more attention than anyone else did.

Not that he should do after all the help he'd given Cornelius.

'What do you mean?' he asked.

Cornelius narrowed his eyes as he stalked up to him.

'I find it interesting that you spoke up first.' Cornelius stared at him, but when Nimrod met his gaze he slapped his shoulder and walked past. 'But then again, I find it interesting that the rest of you are silent.'

The six standing men surrounding Cornelius regrouped, creating an obvious divide with three men standing to one side of their hostage, Yorath Halloway, and the rest moving to the other side. Cornelius walked on to stand behind Yorath.

He leaned on the back of his chair. While looking over Yorath's shoulder, he gestured at Floyd Mercer, telling him to speak.

'In Bigelow Town,' Floyd said with his hands on his hips, 'Riley Weisel told me that the whiskey-soaked lawman Sheriff Lawrence had been shooting his mouth off about us. He said a US marshal is on his way and he's not coming to do no negotiating.'

Several men uttered arrogant laughs.

'Then we'll see him off,' Gilchrist Wheaton, Cornelius's most trusted man, said. 'Yorath's not going nowhere until we get our money.'

'But that's not the worst of it,' Floyd said. 'Lawrence also said that Mayor Halloway had planned to pay us, but that he won't now because he's been told one of us is a Pinkerton detective.'

'That can't be,' Nimrod said, maintaining his stance of being the man who was the most outraged by the news.

'Then how do you explain why they nearly caught us back at the Devil's Hump?' Floyd asked.

Nimrod frowned. In truth the ambush at the Devil's Hump had nothing to do with him.

Despite his faults, Sheriff Lawrence had a lawman's instincts. Using his knowledge of the area, he'd worked out where they'd gone to ground, but with everyone murmuring angrily he reckoned nobody wanted to hear that. He shook his head.

'So now I'll find out who that man is,' Cornelius said, stepping out from behind Yorath. He cast the hostage a sly smile. 'I know it's not you.'

Yorath shook his head and his cheeks stretched as he tried to form a grin behind his gag. He'd been tied up for the two weeks they'd been holed up here. For the first week he'd been obstinate, but now his incarceration had quashed his spirit and he was eager to please.

Yorath was the son of Bigelow Town's mayor and he'd been groomed for political office. He had probably never been tested before and his acceptance of his predicament hadn't impressed Nimrod.

In a strange way Cornelius had impressed him more and he impressed him again when he studied Yorath, clearly looking to see whether his gaze sought out anyone.

Nimrod hadn't made his identity known to Yorath, so he didn't betray him with a guarded eye-flick of the kind that Cornelius was searching for. Cornelius turned to Gilchrist.

'You know it's not me,' Gilchrist said with a wide smile. 'We've known each other since we were children. If I'd wanted to sell you out, I'd have done it years ago.'

'I've always been able to trust my old childhood friend.' Cornelius walked by Gilchrist, then by Wallace and Eddie.

They had stood beside Gilchrist to make the point that they'd also known him for years. 'And I can trust you two, but what about the three men who joined me only recently?'

'You know it's not me,' Floyd said. 'My contact found this out.'

'He did, but Pinkerton detectives are sneaky and you could be trying to cast suspicion elsewhere.' Cornelius waited until Floyd gulped before continuing: 'On the other hand, you're not devious enough to try such a bluff.'

Cornelius swirled round and his gaze picked out the man standing beside Nimrod, Henry Orson.

'I . . . I haven't done nothing,' Henry spluttered. He had been reluctant to join the group and recently his waning enthusiasm had made him behave in an agitated manner. Accordingly, his nervous tone made everyone narrow their eyes. 'I joined you because Halloway double-crossed me on that . . . '

Henry trailed off. He'd told the story several times of the business venture that had failed, leaving him penniless and the mayor with his fortune intact. Rightly, he appeared to judge that telling the tale again might make it sound less plausible than it undoubtedly was.

Slowly Cornelius drew his six-shooter and placed it up beside his cheek. He glanced at it from the corner of his eye as he thumbed back the hammer. Then he lowered the gun to aim it at Henry.

'So is it Henry, who hasn't done nothing and who only joined me to double-cross his boss?' For long moments Cornelius kept the gun on him. Then he jerked it to the side to pick out Nimrod, who had prepared himself for the movement and so managed to avoid reacting. 'Or is it Nimrod, who only joined me for a reason I can't remember now?'

While Henry exhaled his breath loudly in relief, Cornelius searched Nimrod's eyes for a sign that he would go for his own gun, but Nimrod didn't intend to do that. He was outgunned, surrounded, and the moment he reached for his six-shooter he'd be shot to pieces. His only hope was to bluff this out.

So he spread his hands, making an obvious gesture of moving them away from his holster.

'Make your decision carefully, Cornelius,' he said. 'If you get it wrong, we could all get bullets in the back.'

'I'd expect a traitor to make that sort of bluff,' Cornelius said.

Cornelius raised his gun to aim upwards. Then he turned to Henry, who rocked from side to side nervously while gulping, his hand straying towards his holster, but Cornelius moved on until he faced Yorath. He lowered the gun to aim it at him.

'It's not our hostage!' Gilchrist said with a snort of laughter. 'It really isn't.'

'It's not, but if a Pinkerton detective has infiltrated our group, he'll be fearless enough to bluff me out. Even if he's prepared to die, he won't let the man he was trying to save get shot up.'

Cornelius stood side-on to the hostage and sighted his head. He raised his other hand and splayed four fingers and a thumb. 'I'm counting down from five. Then I'm firing.'

'You can't,' Henry said, stepping forward. 'We only did this for the ransom money.'

'I didn't, but don't worry. We'll still get it, and Mayor Halloway will get a holed son in return.'

As Yorath breathed in deeply through his nostrils and closed his eyes, Cornelius stared at Henry until he stepped back. Then Cornelius stiffened his arm and lowered his thumb.

When he bent his smallest finger, Nimrod let out some of his tension with a long breath. His mission was to bring down Cornelius. He hadn't known he'd kidnap Yorath Halloway, but he couldn't let him be killed.

Then again, neither could he save him.

A second finger bent over, and then a third.

Nimrod opened his mouth, a plea on his lips, but he didn't get to utter it when Henry's loud cry echoed in the small room.

'Wait! I don't want him to die. I just want the money I lost.'

Cornelius looked at Henry. Only his index finger was raised and he'd kept the gun levelled on Yorath, who spat out a muffled cry of relief around the gag.

Cornelius shrugged. 'Then you're alone here.'

He bent the finger. Then he fired. The bullet sliced through Yorath's neck.

In an unconscious action, Nimrod reached for his own gun. From the corner of his eye he saw the other men scrambling for their guns, hopefully confusing the situation, but that hope fled when Cornelius swung his gun round to aim it at him.

Nimrod's gun had yet to clear leather, but already he was staring down the barrel of Cornelius's gun.

Nimrod started to shake his head, but then gunfire erupted. Yorath's death had shocked Henry and he hadn't registered that Cornelius had picked Nimrod as being the traitor. He'd gone for his gun, but before he could fire two shots from Floyd and Gilchrist tore into his chest.

Henry stumbled forward for a pace and knocked into Cornelius. Then, in a last desperate act, he thrust out a hand and caught hold of his jacket.

'It wasn't me,' he murmured as he slumped and half-dragged Cornelius down with him.

With Cornelius off balance, Nimrod had only a moment to decide whether he should bluff this out, take everyone on, or run.

He made his decision.

2

'The passing of these two great men is a tragedy for Bigelow Town,' Deputy Trey Thorndike said.

Supportive murmurs drifted around the packed saloon room, a noise that had been heard often over the last three days after Cornelius Lee had come roaring through town. Cornelius had shot up the lawman outside his own law office before dumping the body of Yorath Halloway. These two tragedies had mortified the whole town.

Accordingly, Thorndike glanced at the coffins that stood before the rows of seated people. So many people had wanted to attend the combined funerals of Yorath Halloway and Sheriff Bill Lawrence that the saloon room of the Red Eye had been the only place big enough to cater for them.

Even so, the room had filled up an

hour before the service began and around fifty people had congregated outside. Now they stood on sentinel guard on either side of the open doorway.

Earlier Mayor Halloway had spoken movingly about his son and now Lawrence's deputy was giving his own sombre eulogy.

'I worked for Bill for five years,' Thorndike continued, 'and I'm proud to say that everything I know about being a lawman I learnt from him. To think he won't be around no more is hard to contemplate.'

Thorndike broke off to cough. He nervously rubbed his trim moustache before he continued:

'Certainly a night in here won't be the same without Bill Lawrence around, and Wyndham says his profits are sure to be down.' Thorndike looked up, hoping that his small joke hadn't offended anyone. He smiled when several people nodded knowingly and shuffled on their seats. 'But keeping up with saloon gossip was what . . . was what . . . '

Thorndike trailed off as consternation arose at the back of the gathering. A large man was striding down the centre of the aisle having just come in.

Several men who had been outside were trailing along in his wake. Two of them were limping.

The newcomer was taller than a rodeo bull and twice as angry. He was trail dirty, sported an unkempt bushy beard, and reeked worse than a fly-blown sheep carcass.

He ignored the mourners who were standing to gesture at him to keep back. One man stepped out before him with a raised hand, but the newcomer brushed him aside.

'Gossip,' Thorndike said, raising his voice to distract everyone from watching the disturbance, 'was what — '

'Was what killed him,' the new man said. He stomped to a halt before Lawrence's coffin.

'And who are you to say that?'

'Marshal Devine.'

The marshal looked down at Sheriff Lawrence's body, which was lying in the open coffin. A sheet had been drawn up over his mouth to let just his eyes show, covering up the disfiguring wound Cornelius Lee's bullet had inflicted.

Devine whipped the sheet away. His expression remained impassive as he considered the ruined jaw that the high collar couldn't conceal completely.

He looked up and met Thorndike's gaze. Obligingly Thorndike returned an understanding smile, acknowledging that Lawrence's actions had touched many people over the years and not just in Bigelow Town.

Then he wished he hadn't smiled when Devine jerked his head forward and unleashed a great glob of spit that splattered across the dead man's forehead.

'Why did — ?' Thorndike said, but Devine rounded on him, making his mouth go dry and cutting off his question.

'Lawrence was scum,' Devine muttered. 'He wasn't fit to wear the star.'

He backed away for a pace and then, with a snort of anger, he raised a foot and planted it against the side of the coffin. With a firm shove he kicked it off the low table, spilling the body onto the floor.

The front row of men rose up. Several men hurried over to the body, but most confronted Devine.

'You'll leave now,' Mayor Halloway intoned, leading the complainers.

Devine looked the mayor up and down. He sneered, then pushed him aside.

Halloway went stumbling into two men, who tried to hold him up, but he was moving too quickly and all three men fell over. With clear space opening up Devine stepped over the sprawling men.

Another mourner hurried in and slapped a hand on his shoulder, but he received an elbow in the stomach, making him double over and stagger away. Devine didn't even acknowledge his presence as he ran his gaze over the rows of outraged mourners.

One man on the back row wasn't paying him any attention: Riley Weisel. A thin smile broke Devine's grim visage. Then he strode on down the aisle.

People leapt from their seats to block his way, but he barged them aside easily until he stood before Riley, who studiously fixed his gaze on the men crowding in on Devine from behind.

'Name,' Devine muttered.

Riley slowly turned to Devine, as if he'd somehow only just noticed him.

'Why should I tell you what my — ?'

He didn't get to complete his unhelpful comment; Devine grabbed his jacket and hoisted him to his feet.

'I know your name,' he grunted while glaring at the defiant man, his hot breath rustling his sparse hair. 'Give me a name.'

'I . . . I don't know what you mean.'

Devine drew his Peacemaker and thrust it up under Riley's chin, forcing him to raise his head.

'You told someone Lawrence was shooting his mouth off.'

Riley gulped and shot a glance at Mayor Halloway, who was now making his way through the throng to confront Devine.

'This is an outrage,' Halloway said. 'Today we're marking the passing of two great men. Your investigation can wait.'

'Name,' Devine said, unperturbed. He cocked his gun and thrust it a mite higher, making Riley wince.

'Floyd,' Riley murmured with an audible gulp, 'I told Floyd Mercer.'

'Obliged,' Devine said.

He fired, kicking Riley back and away from him. He glared down at the body, snorted and then walked over it.

As he paced out of the door he began whistling, while back in the saloon cries of complaint erupted.

* * *

'Your report provides little comfort,' Lieutenant Governor Maddox Kingsley said.

Nimrod Dunn conceded this point with a shrug.

'At least you got to read it,' he said. 'The situation was so bad, I didn't think I'd live to write another report.'

'But you did,' Maddox said, peering at Nimrod over the tops of his glasses, 'while Yorath Halloway didn't, although saving him was the reason you were sent to Bigelow Town.'

Nimrod's mission hadn't been to save Yorath's life, but he'd been summoned to the lieutenant governor's office to be berated for his failings and he wasn't going to argue.

After Yorath's death he'd splayed gunfire around the building, hitting only one man, Floyd Mercer. Then, with lead winging around him, he'd leapt through the window and retreated hastily to his horse. And he'd kept going until he'd thrown Cornelius off his trail.

His only success was the one wounded man, but other than that, all he had to show for his weeks of careful monitoring was an accurate account of Cornelius's activities.

'I have no excuses,' Nimrod said with a stiff back and as much dignity as he could manage. 'But I don't reckon I could have changed what happened.'

'Usually reports on failed missions lay the blame elsewhere.' Maddox leaned forward. 'So tell me what you haven't put in the report.'

Nimrod glanced at the chair he'd refused to sit on earlier. He received a brief nod, so he sat.

'I won't speak ill of a dead man who did a lot for Bigelow Town. But the sheriff of Jackson County shouldn't have let the whiskey loosen his tongue so that he revealed details of my mission in a saloon.'

Maddox steepled his fingers and

leaned back in his chair.

'Lawrence *should* be remembered for what he did right and not for what he did wrong, so I'm pleased you didn't write that down. It demonstrates political awareness and a level of discretion I find heartening. Those attributes can help a career.'

Nimrod sensed that Maddox was approaching the crux of this uncomfortable meeting. His pensive smile suggested he wouldn't like the conclusion.

'I have to be discreet to infiltrate outlaw gangs.'

'You do, and until this unfortunate incident your career had been exemplary. Now, through no mistake you've made, it's been tarnished. An influential man's son is dead and people prefer to believe that Sheriff Lawrence was blameless.'

'I can accept that. Those people live in Bigelow Town while I'll move on.'

'But not this time. I still need the services of a Pinkerton detective. So you're returning to Bigelow Town to put this right.'

Nimrod leaned back in his chair to give himself time to think how he could refuse in a way that Maddox would accept.

'I welcome the opportunity, but I infiltrate outlaw gangs, not track them down.'

'Officially your mission will be to bring down Cornelius Lee, but that won't be your actual mission.' Maddox licked his lips as he took another report from his desk and laid it beside Nimrod's. 'This week there was another unfortunate incident in Bigelow Town, this time at the funerals of Sheriff Lawrence and Yorath Halloway. US Marshal Jake T. Devine attended. When he left one man lay dead. That man passed information to Cornelius, but nevertheless it was a killing at a funeral.'

'I hear that death is not uncommon when Devine's around.'

'I hope you don't approve of his

methods. I've heard support from some quarters and I despise it. Now I intend to resolve the matter.' Maddox tapped his fingertips together three times before fixing Nimrod with his firm gaze. 'I want you to kill Marshal Devine.'

Nimrod had been expecting a tough mission, but this revelation took him aback. Thirty seconds passed before he replied, during which time Maddox considered him, his blank expression inscrutable.

'Devine is a US marshal. What you're suggesting is . . . ' Nimrod waved his hands, still struggling to find the right words. He narrowed his eyes. 'Don't do this. If Devine ruffled feathers at a funeral, withdraw his badge the proper way.'

'I can't. Devine always gets his quarry, so even though his career is littered with overreaction and bodies, he has supporters. But times are changing and Devine no longer has a place. And you're the man to stop him.'

'I'm not. Look elsewhere.'

Maddox drew Nimrod's report back to the centre of his desk. Then he placed the report on Devine's activities beside it. He planted a finger on Nimrod's report.

'Your career has two possible directions. In one your activities in Bigelow Town become common knowledge. As a result important people become aggrieved with your failings and your career does this.'

Maddox pushed the report off the end of his desk, scattering the papers.

Nimrod watched the sheets flutter to the floor.

'I understand,' he said when the last one settled.

'Good.' Maddox planted a finger on the second report and drew it closer. 'Because I'd prefer you to take the second option.'

'I said I understood, not that I'd kill a lawman.'

'Spare me the excuses!' Maddox grunted with irritation as he swept the report off his desk. 'Arrange for someone else to dispose of him, if you must. I've read your record. I know the things you've done when you've infiltrated outlaw gangs.'

'They were killers.'

'And so is Devine.' Maddox stood and walked over to Devine's report. He picked it up, then sat on the edge of his desk. 'Our respected governor has announced he won't seek a second term, so next week in Bigelow Town I'll announce my intention to be the new governor. I'll pledge to clean up Jackson County with minimal bloodshed and by ensuring that the guilty face proper legal process. I need Devine out of the way.'

'Your need is wrong.'

'Maybe.' Maddox considered him. 'But the only question that should concern you is: do I need you?'

3

'How may I assist you?' Lucas Brown asked when he'd opened the door set within the gates.

Marshal Devine looked past Lucas and cast his steady gaze around the grounds of the Mission Santa Cruz.

'You patched up a holed man,' he said. 'Bring him.'

'I can't confirm that.' Lucas moved over to block the door. 'Since the monks moved to the Mission San Miguel those of us who have stayed on have continued to help anyone without question.'

Devine narrowed his eyes to streaks of ice.

'Bring Floyd Mercer.'

'You're welcome to share bread and to worship if — '

With a grunt of anger Devine hit Lucas's shoulder with a backhanded swipe that sent him to his knees. Then he brushed past him to look around the mission grounds.

He faced a quadrangle. A chapel was to the right and a row of three squat adobe buildings was to the left.

Devine took the buildings systematically. When he reached the first building he stood beside the only door, listening. He heard no noise within, but he still drew his Peacemaker and then moved in quickly through the open doorway.

The building was empty, presenting a single large room. The second building was identical to the first, but it contained several cots, along with a few belongings.

Devine kicked the bedding and belongings around, but he found nothing to suggest that Floyd had been here.

By the time he was striding along to the third building, Lucas was shuffling across the quadrangle to intercept him. Devine heard voices coming from within the last building, so he waited for him to arrive.

'Who's in there?' he demanded.

Lucas took a deep breath. 'I won't let you treat this mission with disrespect.'

Devine grabbed Lucas's shoulders, spun him round, then shoved him through the doorway. As he didn't draw gunfire, Devine followed him in. Lucas was still reeling as Devine stomped to a halt and looked around the room.

Aside from Lucas, three men were in the room. Two men were tending to a third man, who was lying on a cot.

The patient was feverish, with sweat slicking his face. He gave Devine only a cursory glance before he returned to staring up at the ceiling.

'Floyd Mercer?' Devine said as he paced towards him.

The patient didn't react although the two helpers stood up to face him. Their expressions were calm.

'We won't help you,' Lucas said, joining the two men, 'but we won't stand in your way either.'

To reinforce his point Lucas stood

aside, giving Devine free passage to the cot. Devine still pushed him further away before he loomed over the ill man.

The patient gave a weak cough and licked his cracked lips.

'I've never heard of this man,' he croaked.

Devine nodded and then moved as if to leave, but then he swung back and planted a firm foot against the side of the cot. He kicked it over, making the patient go sprawling. Then he was on him, tearing away his rough blanket.

The other men moved in to help the fallen man, but a harsh glare from Devine made them back away. Then Devine ran his gaze over the patient, but through his damp clothing he couldn't see any bandages.

'Floyd Mercer had lead in him,' Devine said.

Lucas and the other two helpers considered him with their lips clamped firmly shut, but their benign expressions provided most of the answers Devine needed. He still rubbed the sole of his boot over the patient's chest and stomach, receiving only a weak complaint.

Devine kicked the man in the side to be sure he hadn't been wounded, then headed outside. The chapel was the only other building here, so he strode over to it. Lucas hurried after him.

'That man is gravely ill,' he called. 'You caused him unnecessary distress. This must stop.'

Devine came to a halt and swirled round to face him.

'Floyd Mercer!'

Lucas flashed a smile, seemingly seeking common ground.

'I can see you're a determined man, but the chapel is a sacred place. You mustn't violate it.'

'Obliged. Now stay out of my way.'

Lucas gulped, clearly only then realizing that his plea had inadvertently told Devine where his quarry was. Devine resumed his journey to the chapel.

'Please,' Lucas said, hurrying after him, 'people come to pray in the chapel and you must respect that.'

'Praying won't help Floyd where he's going.'

Devine reached the door. He stood against the wall and backhanded it open. Then he slipped through the doorway and moved to the right.

Only one man was within, kneeling before the altar. Bulky bandages swaddled his chest. Low murmuring sounded, suggesting he was praying.

Devine walked down the aisle, his heavy footfalls echoing in the chapel as he made no attempt to mask his passage. Lucas followed him, although at a more sedate pace.

The man looked forward, although he stiffened his back, confirming that he knew he'd been found. His calmness made Devine look around the chapel, but he could see into the corners and nobody else was here.

He stopped behind the praying man, who continued to pray for benediction, although his murmuring grew more insistent in tone. Lucas came around Devine, giving him a wide berth, and moved into the praying man's line of sight.

'You're safe,' he said. 'You have sanctuary in God's house.'

The man nodded, then shuffled round on his knees towards Devine. The moment his gaze picked him out, Devine kicked him in the ribs, knocking him on to his side.

'Wrong!' he roared as the man folded up in pain, clutching his chest.

Devine holstered his gun and grabbed the man's shoulder. Then he drew him to his feet, where he stood hunched over.

'We've only just stitched up his wound,' Lucas said.

'You wasted your time on this low-down skunk.'

Devine punched the man in the guts, dragging a bleat of pain from his lips before he staggered backwards. Only the altar stopped him from falling. Two goblets and a cross went skittering to the floor.

'You can't do this,' Lucas screeched as Devine advanced on the wounded man while drawing back his fist ready to hit him again.

'Then tell me who he is.' Devine stilled his arm.

'He's Floyd Mercer.' Lucas cast Floyd an apologetic glance and took a pace towards Devine. 'But no matter what he's done, anyone can seek solace here. You won't take him from this place.'

'The God man has spoken,' Devine said, stepping up to Floyd. 'So give me what I want here.'

'I don't know what you want,' Floyd spluttered.

'You're a worthless piece of trash who worked for Cornelius Lee. Where is he?'

With a roll of the shoulders Floyd gathered his strength. He straightened. Blood dribbled through his fingers as he clutched his stomach.

'Cornelius is a trusted friend,' he gasped with defiance. 'I'll never sell him out.'

Devine drew his gun and sighted Floyd's bloodied chest.

'Talk or get another hole in the guts.'

'Then shoot. I've made my peace.' Floyd looked at Lucas. 'Thank you for the opportunity.'

As Devine said nothing Lucas moved in and laid a hand on Floyd's shoulder.

'You've always been welcome here.' He gestured at Devine. 'And now the lawman will go. I can't protect you if you leave, but you can stay for as long as you wish.'

'Obliged,' Floyd said. He rubbed his ribs and then glanced at the bloodied hand. 'So go, lawman. You can't do nothing to make me talk.'

Devine glared at Floyd. Slowly he shook his head.

'You got plenty wrong in your miserable life. That was your last mistake.'

Devine firmed his gun hand, making

Lucas pace up to him.

'Leave now,' Lucas said, pointing to the door.

Devine considered Lucas. As a smile spread across Floyd's face in anticipation of Lucas getting his way, Devine swung his gun to the side and shot Lucas in the stomach, making him fall to his knees.

A second bullet to the chest sent him toppling forward to the floor.

Devine lowered his gun into its holster and faced Floyd.

'If I can do that to a God man,' he said, grinning, 'can you imagine what I'll do to you?'

4

'Maddox Kingsley sends me a Pinkerton detective,' Mayor Halloway said, 'when I need a dozen lawmen to flush out Cornelius Lee.'

'I'd heard that a lawman is already around,' Nimrod said. He watched Halloway's reaction closely, although he didn't need any special skills to interpret the irate politician's opinion.

Halloway waved an angry hand at him before he walked to the window to peer down at the road below. After a few moments he turned back to consider him over his desk.

'The last thing I need is Marshal Devine rounding him up. If his performance at my son's funeral is typical, more good citizens will die in the crossfire than would from Cornelius's actions.'

'If I've understood it right, the man

Devine shot was passing information on to Cornelius.'

Halloway accepted this comment with a reluctant nod, but that didn't stop him from going on to pour more scorn on Devine and his brutal methods. Nimrod encouraged him to speak his mind, hoping the mayor's opinion would help him to resolve his own dilemma.

Reluctantly he had agreed to accept Maddox Kingsley's mission to kill Devine, even though it was a secret one that nobody else, including his superiors, knew about. But his acceptance didn't mean he had to complete it.

In his missions he got close to his targets. While he'd been with Cornelius Lee he'd learnt that he was unlike the usual outlaw. He was shrewd and he had a plan, of which the kidnapping of the mayor's son was only a part, but he had discussed that plan only with those closest to him.

Strangest of all, until the mission had ended in violence, he had done nothing to suggest his reputation as a ruthless outlaw was warranted.

Despite this, nothing Nimrod had learnt would have dissuaded him from killing Cornelius, and he had resolved to do the same on this mission. He would find Devine and join him on his mission to track down Cornelius.

While they worked together, he would study Devine and see if Maddox's, and now Halloway's, anger justified killing a US marshal. Unlike with Cornelius, he would need some convincing that it did.

'He violated a funeral,' Halloway said, repeating himself as his tirade ran out of steam. 'If one of the mourners had killed him the whole town would have rejoiced, and I'd have protected that man from reprisals.'

'Perhaps one day soon,' Nimrod said levelly, 'someone will take matters into their own hands.'

Halloway's eyes glazed as he contemplated the welcome possibility.

'Maybe,' he said using the same

guarded tone as Nimrod's.

'So you'll be comforted to hear that despite the poor reputation many of our operatives have, I'll employ more acceptable methods than Devine uses.'

'That's only half the problem.' Halloway sat and considered Nimrod before he continued. 'The rumour that got my son killed was that a Pinkerton detective had infiltrated Cornelius's gang. Can you confirm that?'

'I can confirm that was the rumour.'

Anger flashed in Halloway's eyes before he leapt to his feet. He slapped both hands on his desk and leaned over it to glare at Nimrod.

'Don't toy with me. Cornelius killed my son and I'll make him suffer before he hangs for his crimes, but I'm saving my worst for the operative who stood by and let Yorath die. When this sorry affair is over I'll have a name and that man's head.'

Nimrod was thankful that he was adept at brazening out tough situations. He returned Halloway's gaze with an understanding smile while he spread his hands in a show of sympathy.

'I'm sorry about Yorath, but I don't know if anyone was trying to get close to Cornelius. The nature of the work means that we don't know what other operatives are doing.'

Halloway accepted his answer with a snarl before he headed back to the window to look out.

'So I must place the fate of my town into the hands of a Pinkerton detective while hoping that no more of my good citizens end up dead at the hands of a renegade marshal.' Halloway raised a hand to the wall. He leaned forward as he watched three men dismount outside the saloon opposite and then walk across the road towards his office. He lowered his tone to a more conciliatory one. 'How I can help you find Cornelius?'

'Anything you can tell me would help.' The stern set of Halloway's shoulders made Nimrod wonder if it would be wise to ask about something that had puzzled him. But he figured that this meeting would probably be a short one and he shouldn't prevaricate. 'Cornelius's ransom demand was five thousand dollars. You're a wealthy man and yet instead of paying him you posted a bounty of the same amount on his head.'

Halloway turned and shrugged. 'You don't do the bidding of men like Cornelius Lee. You defy them. My son would have understood that, even if you don't.'

Yorath hadn't understood. When they'd received the news, he'd wailed and pleaded for Cornelius not to kill him. He'd been so annoying that Cornelius had gagged him.

'I'd have thought the more important thing was to save Yorath's life. Afterwards, you could have captured Cornelius and reclaimed the money.'

Halloway ground his teeth, a retort clearly on his lips, but when he regained his composure he nodded to the door.

'You've wasted enough of my time. I

have important people to see.'

'We'll meet again,' Nimrod said, mulling over Halloway's reaction. 'I hope I'll have more encouraging news then.'

Nimrod headed to the door, but Halloway must have given an unnoticed signal as, before he reached it, the door swung open.

The three men Halloway had watched crossing the road stood in the corridor. They came straight in, but they stopped beside the door to appraise him. All three men sported lively grins, arrogant stances and tied-down holsters.

Nimrod avoided their gazes as he moved to walk between them, but two men closed ranks to ensure he couldn't get by without barging into their shoulders. Nimrod avoided the possible confrontation by stopping.

He looked at the man who hadn't moved, then raised his hat while planting a pleasant smile on his face.

The man considered his placid demeanour. Then he returned the smile and flicked his gaze to the others.

When they moved aside, Nimrod left. Behind him he heard a murmured comment that made the others laugh, but it had been uttered too quietly for him to hear the words. He still stopped in the corridor to show that he'd heard before he carried on.

The last thing he heard as the door closed was Halloway asking the men to join him in a drink. Only when he was outside on the boardwalk did he realize he'd seen one of the men before.

'Sheridan Cox,' he said, 'bounty hunter.'

* * *

'You failed to find Cornelius Lee when I put five thousand dollars on his head,' Mayor Halloway said, nursing his glass against his chest, 'so what makes you confident you can find him when I've doubled the bounty?'

'Cornelius had gone to ground,' Sheridan Cox said, shrugging. 'Now he's running. He'll leave a trail. We'll follow it.'

'Cornelius had gone to ground with my son, who is now dead. Don't forget that.'

'We won't. Avenging the tragic death of that noble young man is the only reason we're here.' Sheridan took a swig of whiskey and then chuckled. 'Along with the money.'

As the other two men, Mason Philips and Nash Taylor, laughed with their leader, Halloway took a deep breath.

'The worst thing about this is dealing with men like you.'

Sheridan glanced at the door, seemingly unconcerned with the insult.

'Did the man who left also go off in search of ten thousand dollars?'

'Perhaps.' Halloway leaned back in his chair, relishing his reply for the first time since his distasteful guests had arrived. 'So this time you'd better act quickly.'

'We will, and he might give us a place to start.'

'He knows less than you do, as if that's possible.' Halloway waited for another surly retort, but Sheridan stayed quiet. 'So is there anything you need to know?'

'Nope. The next time you see us, we'll be dragging Cornelius Lee's body into town.'

Halloway nodded. He waited while Sheridan placed his empty glass on his desk and turned to go before he raised a hand, halting him.

'You've misunderstood my instructions. I've doubled the bounty because the task will be twice as hard.' He leaned forward. 'I want Cornelius Lee alive.'

For the first time that Halloway had seen, Sheridan Cox was lost for words.

* * *

The Mission Santa Cruz appeared deserted.

Nimrod had followed Marshal Devine's path around the county

easily. Numerous people had seen a large and determined man passing by. Most of those who had answered Devine's questions sported bruises and they either ran away when he tried to talk to them, or they reckoned he should turn back while he still could.

Nimrod rode through the open gates without being approached. The quadrangle was silent.

He rode past the chapel and investigated the three buildings first. The first two were empty, but when he reached the door to the third building buzzing flies warned him about what he would find.

Nimrod entered and paced around the single room, finding that only one man had died here. As that man was lying in a cot with his face swollen and contorted, it was likely that he had died of an illness, albeit combined with neglect.

In a pensive mood Nimrod walked to the chapel. Again, at the door buzzing flies told him what was within. He slipped in through the open door and stood with his back to the wall, surveying the scene.

His gaze darted about, unsure which horror to dwell on first.

A man lay in the aisle, sprawled on his chest in a sticky dark pool. Another man lay over a pew, his back arched and his arms dangling. A neat hole in the forehead testified as to his fate as a similar wound did for another man who lay curled up beside the altar.

Nimrod paced down the aisle, glancing into all corners of the chapel, confirming that whoever had done this had gone, but when he reached the altar, there was one more horror to find.

The cross that must have stood behind the altar had been chopped down. On it lay Floyd Mercer. His hands and feet had been nailed to the wood in a terrible recreation of the crucifixion.

His chest had been sliced open to spill his guts onto the floor. His mouth had opened so wide in what would now be an eternal, silent scream, that it looked as if his jaw had been broken, suggesting he had been alive through his torment.

Floyd had been an outlaw, but Nimrod still bowed his head. Then he removed a cloth from the altar and placed it over his body. As he could find nothing to give the others dignity, he drew them up before the altar in a line.

He took one last look at the scene to imprint it on his mind for the moment when he caught up with the perpetrators, then he turned to the door. Shaking his head in anger at the depths men can plumb, he put his mind to who had done this.

When he reached the door he considered the men who had been with Cornelius and wondered if they had been capable of committing this atrocity, or if any of them had a personal hatred of Floyd Mercer.

'Who could have done this?' he said to himself as he headed outside.

A heavy footfall sounded behind him a moment before cold steel slapped into the side of his neck.

'Marshal Devine,' a harsh voice muttered in his ear.

5

'Marshal Jake T. Devine,' Nimrod said, glimpsing the large lawman from the corner of the eye, 'don't shoot. I've come to help you.'

'Nobody helps me,' Devine muttered. 'Now why shouldn't I splatter your brains over the church door?'

Nimrod took a deep breath. 'I'm a Pinkerton detective.'

Devine snorted. 'Bad try. I kill those with my bare hands.'

Nimrod gulped, thinking for a moment that Devine would be true to his word, but with a snort of disgust the marshal lowered his gun. Nimrod stepped back for a pace and nodded into the church.

'You figured out yet who did that?'

Devine narrowed his eyes. 'I don't help no Pinkerton man.'

He headed off towards the nearest

building. Nimrod watched him walk away, the thought coming that he could complete his mission by just drawing his gun and shooting the marshal in the back. But, almost as if Devine had overheard the thought, he glanced over his shoulder at him.

With a sigh Nimrod hurried after him.

'We should share information,' Nimrod said when he joined the marshal.

'I'm not interested in what you know,' Devine said. 'Get out of my sight.'

'So the location of Cornelius Lee's hideout doesn't interest you, then?' Nimrod turned away. 'I'll investigate that on my own. Don't follow me.'

Devine's gaze burnt the back of his neck, but he'd tried his guess that rude retorts were the only way to find common ground with him, so he went to his horse. When he'd mounted up he saw that the marshal had collected his big bay, which he must have left behind the chapel.

The two men rode towards the gates, taking diagonal courses across the quadrangle that closed on each other, although when they were twenty yards away, Devine speeded to reach the gates first.

Outside the mission grounds Devine turned to the right, this being the correct way to go, so Nimrod moved on to draw alongside.

'Where?' Devine said.

'The original mission building five miles on beside the creek.'

'How do you know that, Pinkerton man?'

'I infiltrated Cornelius Lee's outlaw gang. That's where we holed up.'

Devine swirled round in the saddle to glare at him, his eyes blazing.

'You rode with that snake and you let him live!' He bunched his fists. 'That's why I hate you Pinkerton men. You don't get friendly with outlaws. You blast them to hell.'

'And I would have when I'd learnt about Cornelius's activities, except I didn't get the chance. Sheriff Lawrence talked and I barely got out of there alive.'

'You deserved to die,' Devine spat. He moved his horse on to get ahead.

Nimrod considered hurrying after him, but Devine slowed when he had fifty yards on him, so Nimrod followed on behind at his own pace. They didn't speak again on the journey.

At the old hideout Devine took his horse around the small, squat building to consider it from all angles before he dismounted. He ignored Nimrod as he headed inside.

Nimrod noted the broken window through which he'd leapt. Then he went in after Devine to find that the room where he and Cornelius had holed up for two weeks had been cleaned out.

The only evidence he could find to show that anyone had ever been here was a dark stain on the dusty floor, where Yorath's body had fallen. When he knelt to finger the area, Devine noted his interest and stood over him.

'Yorath,' Nimrod said simply.

'You stood by while the man you were protecting died,' Devine muttered with contempt.

Nimrod pointed to other, smaller stains.

'That's probably Henry Orson; Cornelius finished him off. And that could be Floyd Mercer. I winged him before I hightailed it out of here.'

'Leaving him and the rest alive.'

'It didn't do Floyd any good from the look of what happened to him back there.'

Devine kicked dust over the stains and then paced around the room.

'On the other hand, if you weren't a yellow-belly, he wouldn't have blabbered about your friend Cornelius.'

Nimrod ran Devine's comment back through his mind to check that he'd heard him right.

'Are you saying you nailed him to the cross?'

Devine rubbed his bushy beard. 'It felt like a good idea at the time.'

'And the other dead men?'
'Got in my way.'

Devine cast him a sideways glance. Then he kicked open the only internal door to reveal another empty room.

Nimrod watched him hurl discarded items of clothing around, wondering whether, despite Devine's reputation, he had made a joke, but he judged that the marshal wouldn't avoid the truth.

'They were God-fearing men who stayed at the mission to help others,' Nimrod said when Devine returned to the main room, shock making his voice crack.

'They colluded with your friend.' Devine gestured around the room. 'Someone emptied this place. The furniture is in the mission.'

Nimrod lowered his head as he cast his mind back.

Devine was right. The crude furniture that had been in here was now in one of the mission buildings. Also, Floyd used to fetch their food, but he'd always returned to the hideout quickly, so the men at the mission probably had helped Cornelius, presumably through fear.

He nodded, but that didn't change one fact.

'You've never been here before,' he said, looking up. 'You couldn't have known that for sure until I confirmed it.'

'I'm a US marshal, not a Pinkerton man.'

Devine made for the door. As there was nothing else to uncover here, Nimrod followed.

'Perhaps we can still pick up a trail,' he said, hurrying on to catch up with Devine.

'I learnt everything I need to know in there.'

'Which is?'

Devine stopped to look him up and down. He snorted.

'I ride alone, Pinkerton man.'

With that, Devine turned away and walked towards his horse.

Nimrod settled his stance, accepting that Devine's overreaction at the mission had made it easy for him. He reckoned he'd get a clear shot at Devine's back when the marshal was riding away, but like before, as if he'd picked up on his thoughts, when Devine mounted up he looked at him.

For the first time that Nimrod had seen, Devine smiled.

* * *

'Cornelius Lee,' Sheridan Cox said, leaning on the bar.

'Never heard of him,' the bartender of the Dark Moon said with studied indifference.

'He comes to Lone Star when there's trouble, and then he causes a whole heap more.'

The bartender considered him. 'You a friend of his?'

'Sure.'

'Then I definitely don't know where he is.'

The bartender held his gaze. Then he flicked his gaze to the stairs and briefly held up three fingers before he converted the motion into drying a glass with a towel.

Sheridan didn't register that he'd seen the signal; instead he drank his whiskey with his two companions, Mason and Nash.

After their meeting with Mayor Halloway the three men had gone straight to Lone Star, ensuring that they got ahead of Nimrod Dunn, who had ridden off in search of Marshal Devine.

Sheridan reckoned that no matter what clues those men picked up, they would ultimately look for Cornelius in Lone Star, the most lawless town in Jackson county, and a town that had resisted anyone's attempts to clean it up.

When they'd downed their drinks the three men headed to the stairs. Sheridan noted that several drinkers guardedly watched their every step, but he wasn't unduly worried; in a town like Lone Star, everyone acted suspiciously.

He went up the stairs first with Mason and Nash traipsing along behind. At the third room he stopped beside the door and waited until everyone was in position. Then he stretched out an arm.

Before he could rap on the door, shuffling sounded within. Then a voice spoke up from behind the door and to the right.

'Come in.'

Sheridan swung round to face the door, raised his hands to shoulder level, then put on a wide smile. He nodded to Nash, who pushed the door open.

Slowly the door swung away to reveal a window facing him and then a bed, but no people. Unperturbed, Sheridan paced forward and, as the rest of the room came into view, he saw three men sitting on chairs with their backs to the walls. Last of all he saw Cornelius Lee sitting in the corner, with his gun levelled on him.

'You alone?' Cornelius asked.

'Nope.' Sheridan gestured and Nash

and Mason followed him in, both men matching his posture of keeping their hands raised.

'So you're the first ones to find me,' Cornelius said.

'It wasn't hard,' Sheridan said.

Cornelius accepted this point with a smile, his reaction encouraging his men to laugh.

Sheridan used the break to look around and note that everyone had drawn their guns, although unlike Cornelius they were keeping them lowered.

'And now that you're here,' Cornelius said, 'what do you plan to do?'

'I intend to take you prisoner, escort you back to Bigelow Town, and claim the bounty Mayor Halloway has put on your hide.' Sheridan winked. 'He wants you alive.'

Cornelius whistled through his teeth. 'That's the first sensible thing he's done in a while.'

'And so,' Sheridan said, lowering his hands slowly, 'the question is: am I the man who'll collect that bounty?'

6

After Nimrod had returned to bury the bodies at the Mission Santa Cruz he resumed tracking west. He didn't catch sight of Marshal Devine again and he didn't try to pick up his tracks.

He didn't need to. He was sure he'd go to Lone Star, the source of most of the trouble that came Bigelow Town's way.

The sun was lowering when he rode into Lone Star, but to his surprise he discovered that Devine hadn't come here. Nobody had seen a large lawman recently and Nimrod reckoned Devine didn't arrive anywhere quietly.

So he worked his way around the saloons, drinking lightly, gently probing for news, and seeking out familiar faces.

Although he'd been holed up with Cornelius Lee in only two hideouts, other men had occasionally helped them or arrived with news. He looked for these men, and when he found one it turned out to be Jerome Malleson, one of Cornelius's closest confidants, who was drinking alone in the Dark Moon.

Nimrod had already been served, so he took his whiskey to a quiet corner and, in his usual secretive way, he watched him from the corner of his eye.

Jerome was also being watchful. He was peering around, noticing newcomers, although he dropped no hints that he had been watchful enough to recognize Nimrod. On the other hand Nimrod wouldn't expect Jerome to be looking for him.

After an hour of this behaviour Jerome pushed away from the bar and headed to the stairs. His steady perusal of the crowded saloon room before he mounted the stairs neither sought out Nimrod nor made an obvious show of ignoring him. Jerome wasn't a sneaky man, so when he reached the top of the stairs, in a confident frame of mind

Nimrod followed.

Jerome turned down the corridor to disappear from view. Nimrod followed at a steady pace, trying to avoid appearing suspicious to anyone who was watching him from below.

When he reached the top of the stairs, a door creaked open and, when he saw the corridor, the third door down was closing, although when it stopped moving it left a gap.

As he was now out of view from the saloon room, Nimrod hurried along, using light steps to reach the door. He waited, listening.

Jerome was rummaging around inside, so, with his gun drawn, Nimrod moved to open the door, aiming to burst in and surprise him.

His free hand had touched the wood when the door was thrown open to reveal Jerome. He had an arrogant gleam in his eye that showed he had known he was being followed.

With a quick motion he chopped a hand down on Nimrod's wrist, making him drop his gun. Then he grabbed his arm and swung him into the room and to the bed. When he came to rest, Jerome had pressed his face down into the bedspread and had thrust a six-shooter into the back of his neck.

'You were patient down there,' Jerome muttered in his ear, 'but I was more patient, Nimrod Dunn, if that's your real name.'

'I'm Nimrod,' he said, his voice muffled. 'I never lied about that.'

'And the rest?'

Nimrod had memorized detailed cover stories that he could use if his stated role was doubted, but with a gun against his neck he needed a more direct approach.

'I joined Cornelius for the money, but then again, so did others. Now heaps of people are on his trail and I'm the only one who can save his life, and yours.'

'How?'

'Don't go to the Mission Santa Cruz. A US marshal has been there. He's killed everyone.'

Jerome's hand relaxed slightly. 'I didn't know that.'

'You could be the next man Marshal Devine shoots up, or for that matter me and anyone else who gets in his way.' Nimrod paused before he made his offer. 'But maybe the two of us can take him on.'

Jerome snorted, conveying the unlikely possibility of his agreeing to this, but he did raise the gun and then drag Nimrod up from the bed.

'What's your plan?' he asked when he'd stood him up against the wall.

'I don't have one, but let me speak to Cornelius. I'll explain myself and let him decide if he wants me back.'

'Cornelius gave you all the answers you need when he sent you running with hot lead burning your heels.' Jerome narrowed his eyes. 'You have no idea what's going on, do you? You're just another rat sniffing around hoping to get your hands on Cornelius's hard work.'

'Then tell me what's happening.'

'Cornelius didn't trust you enough to explain, so I sure won't.'

Nimrod lowered his head as he considered, but he couldn't think of a way to make Jerome talk. When he looked up, Jerome was looking at the door with an ear cocked.

Jerome was nervous and yet, when Nimrod had met him before, he'd been confident. Something had gone wrong and it wasn't just that people were chasing him. He also couldn't take him to Cornelius because he didn't know where he'd gone.

Nimrod caught all this in a momentary consideration of Jerome's furtive gaze before Jerome gathered a firmer grip of his jacket and moved him into a position where he could watch both him and the door. A few moments later footfalls sounded outside as someone came down the corridor.

Jerome muttered under his breath, then aimed his gun at the door.

Nimrod made him pay for his

decision. He shoved forward. Then he grabbed Jerome's gun arm and pushed it above his head. The motion squeezed out a shot that wasted itself into the ceiling.

A warning cry went up in the corridor outside followed by a demand for help. The voice had sounded scared, suggesting that whoever had come upstairs had done so innocently, but that wouldn't be the case for whoever responded.

The Dark Moon employed men to quell trouble, and they did it quickly and ruthlessly.

In the room the two men struggled, their attempts to wrestle the gun downwards walking them away from the wall and then towards the window.

Nimrod put two hands to Jerome's wrist, but Jerome wrapped his free hand around Nimrod's wrist; so they faced a stalemate with the gun circling but always remaining aimed straight up.

Rapid approaching footfalls sounded outside and this encouraged Jerome to redouble his efforts. The gun swung in towards Nimrod's head; Nimrod raised himself.

He used his small height advantage to stop the gun's progress, then he kept it held firmly a foot above his head. Then he removed a hand from Jerome's wrist and hammered a short-armed jab into Jerome's stomach.

The blow landed without much force, but with Jerome straining to lower the gun, it blasted the air from his lungs and he doubled over. The gun swung down past Nimrod's shoulder.

With only a moment to act before Jerome regained his strength, Nimrod removed his other hand and delivered an upward backhanded slap to the cheek that sent his opponent reeling. He followed through with a second, firmer blow to the chin that knocked him towards the window.

At the last moment Jerome saw where he was heading. He thrust out a hand to still his progress, but the hand hit the centre of the glass pane and he crashed through it, to fold over the sill and land on the balcony outside.

The footfalls stopped outside the door and a quick muttered debate took place. Nimrod didn't wait for its verdict and he followed Jerome. He used a chair to brush away glass shards and then stepped over the sill onto the balcony.

Jerome had his back to him, his form folded over the balcony rail as he struggled to stop himself falling to the ground below. He braced himself and then looked up, but it was only to find that Nimrod was on him.

He grabbed Nimrod's wrist and this time he managed to tear the gun away from his grip. Nimrod backed away for a pace.

'Where's Cornelius?' he said.

'I'm not telling you — '

A gunshot roared from within the room and, without making a sound, Jerome clutched his bloodied side and then fell over the rail.

From his position to the side of the

window Nimrod couldn't see into the room, but as whoever had fired was unlikely to listen to his excuses, he put a foot to the rail. He clambered over it and lowered himself down the other side until he was dangling.

He dropped and landed on the ground beside Jerome's supine form. Few people were about, so Nimrod knelt beside him.

Jerome was breathing, but it was ragged and the spreading bloom of blood on his vest front said he was unlikely to live for long.

'Whoever shot you is now after me,' Nimrod said.

'Don't matter none to me,' Jerome breathed. 'At least I'll die here and not at his hands.'

'Who?'

Jerome hunched his back while murmuring in pain. Then he thrust out a hand and grabbed his collar.

'Mayor Halloway,' he grunted, drawing him closer. 'Don't trust him.'

He dropped down to lie on his back,

where he uttered a prolonged gargling sigh. Above, two men came to the rail and peered down into the road looking for him. Nimrod slipped back to the wall beneath the balcony.

The men on the balcony exchanged views. They decided that one man had got away, but they didn't know who he was.

When they'd clambered back into the room, with a shiver Nimrod made for the shadows. He hurried along the boardwalk and then to the dark alley beside the Dark Moon.

The stables where he'd left his horse were towards the edge of town, but that was across the road and he didn't welcome the thought of running over open ground. So he worked his way around the backs of the buildings on the saloon side of the road to reach the edge of town.

Then he scurried back towards the stables while keeping in the shadows and looking out for signs of pursuit. Thankfully he saw and heard nothing other than the usual milling around and rowdy activity he'd expect in Lone Star.

When he caught his first sight of the stables he saw the reason why he hadn't been pursued. Two men were standing on either side of the large double doors and they were looking from side to side as they clearly waited for him.

Nimrod winced, then moved to go back the way he'd come, but his sudden change of direction caught the attention of the nearer man, who beckoned to the other. Nimrod turned and walked away with what he hoped was a nonchalant gait.

When he glanced over his shoulder the men were following him, matching his speed.

Nimrod gave up on his pretence of innocence and broke into a run. He passed a darkened building and made a quick right, skirted around the side, then doubled back seeking to approach the stables from a different direction.

He ran through a long patch of darkness, but when he was again getting close to the stables a large man stepped out before him, thirty feet ahead, his form shrouded in the shadows. Nimrod skidded to a halt and turned to find that his two pursuers were closing in on him from behind.

He turned back, aiming to confront the solitary man, and caught a flash of gunmetal. He jerked to the side while throwing his hand to his holster, but he'd yet to complete the motion when he recognized his apparent opponent.

The man wasn't pursuing him; the formidable shape was that of Marshal Devine.

Two rapid explosions of light burst from Devine's gun. Behind him two thuds sounded. Then Devine moved on and without comment he breezed by him.

Presently two more shots sounded as Devine ensured that his pursuers were dead. Then he swung round and joined Nimrod.

'I thought you'd come here,' Nimrod said, figuring that Devine wouldn't welcome being thanked.

'Pinkerton men think too much,' Devine said.

'Either way, it seems we're riding together, after all.'

'Sure.' Devine snorted. 'You're good for drawing gunfire.'

7

'Enjoying that?' Devine asked.

'Sure.' Nimrod gnawed off a mouthful of his salted beef and then smiled while he chewed to disguise how tough the old meat had become.

Devine leaned forward to the fire and removed the stick on which was skewered a sizzling jack rabbit. He tore off a leg and watched the juice drip before he chewed a mouthful with relish.

'Do Pinkerton men not eat fresh meat?' he asked with his mouth full.

Nimrod held up his strip of beef. 'We're prepared for any eventuality.'

'Preparation is no use when the man you're protecting gets shot up.'

Nimrod chewed while feeling strangely elated that Devine was trying to rile him so soon after they'd joined forces.

'That was my first mistake on that mission, but I accept full responsibility for it.'

Devine chewed through the second leg before replying.

'In my line of work the first mistake can be the last.'

'And in mine, but this time I've got a second chance. I intend to use it when we return to Lone Star.'

'Not going back.' Devine scratched his bushy beard and reclaimed a fallen scrap of meat. 'Your outlaw friend's not there.'

'How do you know that?'

'You're not filled with lead.'

Nimrod glanced away accepting that Devine wasn't paying him a compliment about his survival instincts.

'I didn't think you'd let someone else ride into town alone and take the bigger risk.'

'Don't care what you think as long as you take the bullets instead of me.'

'And where will I next take the bigger risk?'

'The Mission San Miguel.'

'So you're planning to shoot up defenceless monks this time, are you?'

Devine conceded his question with an unconcerned shrug and sucked the last of the meat from the thigh bone.

'If they don't talk.'

'About what?'

Devine shook his head. 'You infiltrated your friend's outlaw gang, spent weeks with him, and yet you know nothing.'

'My work requires patience. A man who gets all his answers at the end of a gun won't understand that.'

Devine pointed at him with a cleaned bone.

'That's the first thing you've said I've understood. Floyd Mercer trusted the mission men. So they knew your friend had holed up nearby. If he holed up with one group of God men, he'll do it again.'

'He won't. Cornelius isn't that predictable.'

'The day I take the advice of a

Pinkerton man is the day I die.'

Nimrod couldn't stop himself from giving an ironic smile.

'You have nothing but contempt for us. So when have you met our operatives before?'

Devine laughed and tore the remainder of the rabbit in two. He gestured at Nimrod with one half as he talked.

'Was tearing into a no-good bunch of outlaws in the Ozarks when one of them started shooting the others up. Seen that before. When it gets tough, the snakes bite each other, but this time the shooter claimed he was a Pinkerton man sent in to infiltrate the gang.'

Devine tore off a strip of meat, but he didn't eat it as he awaited Nimrod's response.

'What did you do?' Nimrod asked, although he reckoned he knew the answer.

'Ignored his prattle and saved him until last.' Devine pointed at his neck. 'I throttled him, holding him real close so I could spit in his eye.'

Nimrod concentrated on not blinking. 'And was he an outlaw?'

A momentary darkness clouded Devine's eyes before he regained his grim humorous mood by wolfing down the strip of meat.

'He was a Pinkerton man.'

'And how did that make you feel, knowing you'd got it wrong?'

Devine's eyes narrowed again, proving that the taunt that he'd been wrong annoyed him the most.

'I'm always right. You don't infiltrate. You face the scum head-on.'

Nimrod ate the last of his dried meat to avoid showing a reaction.

'We both take the risk that we'll meet someone who's faster with a gun than he is at thinking, but I still reckon our methods are better.'

'I'm alive. Your Pinkerton friend's dead.'

'But was the mission successful?'

'It was,' Devine said, lowering his voice, that being the most acknowledgement he appeared to be willing to provide that Nimrod had made a valid point. 'And this one will be too, using my methods.'

'Mine have a place too. I know how Cornelius thinks.' Nimrod paused to let Devine ridicule him, but he gnawed his rabbit carcass instead. 'He's like no outlaw I've ever met. He's shrewd and not prone to violence, except when it's necessary. Then he's ruthless. He had a bigger plan than just kidnapping the mayor's son and he's probably still working on it. To catch him, you'll have to change your usual tactics.'

'Never,' Devine spluttered through a mouthful of meat.

'You will, and you'll start tomorrow. You won't mistreat the mission monks, even if they've been forced into helping an outlaw.'

Devine smiled. 'If you stand in my way, I'll kill you.'

'And if you stand in my way, I'll kill you.'

Devine tossed the last of the carcass into the fire. As the fat sizzled, he stared at him through the flames. He began whistling tunelessly.

* * *

The Mission San Miguel had the same layout as the Mission Santa Cruz, with a walled area within which stood a chapel and other buildings that were in a state of disrepair.

Nimrod and Devine circled around the perimeter and found that there were no buildings close by, so, if Cornelius had holed up here, he hadn't used the same policy as the last time.

They headed to the gate with Devine leading. Devine waited for someone to greet them, but when nobody appeared, he cast Nimrod a knowing look, as if this somehow proved the monks were up to no good.

Then he dismounted and paced along beside the wall. Nimrod followed him and they worked their way round to a point where disrepair had allowed a section of the wall to fall over.

Devine stopped, although when Nimrod caught up with him, he saw that he was listening and not waiting for him.

The wheeze of the wind as it rustled the dust was the only sound. Devine clambered over the rubble and then darted to the side to stand with his back to the wall.

He stood for only a moment before his gaze centred on the nearest cover, fifty yards away, of a larger section of wall that had collapsed intact. Quickly he hurried over to it and dropped down out of view.

At the same quick pace Nimrod joined him. He peered over a rock and considered the grounds.

'The horses over there aren't Cornelius's,' Nimrod said, pointing.

Devine didn't reply. He stood and then, walking sideways with the wall at his back, he headed to the chapel.

Nimrod adopted a defensive walk, covering the area of the wall that Devine couldn't see. They reached the chapel without seeing anyone.

'If your friend's here,' Devine said, considering the seemingly empty buildings facing the chapel, 'he's hiding.'

'Cornelius holed up at the Devil's Hump for three days until Sheriff Lawrence flushed him out. He's patient.'

'Sheriff Lawrence flushed him out! Your friend impresses me less the more I hear about him.'

Devine moved to enter the chapel. Nimrod advanced quickly and stood beside him.

'I'll do the questioning,' he said. 'I'll get answers and leave them alive.'

'If there's answers, they'll all die.' Devine kicked open the door. Then he walked in and moved to the side.

Nimrod followed him in and, while keeping low, he moved off in the opposite direction. When he knelt behind the end pew and considered the interior, he found that his caution hadn't been needed. The monks were the only people here.

At the front, three robed men were kneeling before a fourth man. A mass was in progress.

'I'm Marshal Devine,' Devine roared, his voice echoing in the chapel as he set off towards them. 'Give me Cornelius Lee.'

Nimrod sighed and looked aloft as the standing monk flinched and then looked up to face the advancing marshal.

'Visitors are always welcome here,' he said. 'I'm Father Goodwin and once I've completed — '

'I want Cornelius Lee!'

Nimrod hurried after Devine, catching up with him as he reached the end of the aisle and loomed over the three kneeling monks, none of whom looked up from their prayers despite his loud and rude interruption.

'I've heard of this man,' Goodwin said, 'but he's not here.'

'You have nothing to fear from Cornelius,' Nimrod said in a soft voice before Devine could retort, 'or from us.

If Cornelius threatened you, we'll protect you, but we must know if he's been here.'

Goodwin placed the candle he was clutching on the altar behind him, a delaying action with which Nimrod was familiar and which he assumed Devine would have noticed too. Then the monk shook his head.

'Check out his story,' Devine grunted.

When Nimrod didn't move Devine shoved him towards the door with a heavy hand that forced him to grab hold of a pew to avoid falling over.

'I've not finished asking my questions yet.'

'Check that your friend isn't here and then ask them.' Devine stepped back to consider him, the movement knocking over one of the kneeling monks, although Devine didn't register that he'd touched him. 'You wanted us to work together. Do it.'

Nimrod frowned, accepting that Devine had thrown down a challenge to see if he would leave him, so that the marshal could interrogate the monks alone. As Nimrod reckoned he wouldn't resort to violence quickly, he smiled at Father Goodwin, who was nervously considering Devine.

'Then work with me,' he said, giving Devine a long stare. Then he backed away down the aisle.

Goodwin started to explain that there was no need to search, but Nimrod turned away. He didn't look back as he walked to the door.

Outside, he put his mind to the task. He hadn't understated Cornelius's ability to hole up quietly, but he had the advantage of knowing about the kind of places he favoured. So he backtracked around the chapel and then walked over to the back of the row of squat buildings.

Small windows looked out, so he worked his way along, listening at each window and then risking a glance inside, but the buildings all proved to be empty until he reached the last one.

Only furniture was within and the sparse furnishing showed that the monks lived here, but Nimrod still investigated; he found a second room that had been occupied recently.

Stale food lay on the floor and bedding had been scattered as if the occupants had left in a hurry. As the monks kept the main room tidy it was likely that whoever had been here didn't live at the mission.

He searched and found no clues as to who these people were, but four cots had been occupied, the number of men who were left in Cornelius Lee's gang.

In a pensive frame of mind, he returned to the chapel. This information would make Devine overreact, but as he couldn't keep it from him, he hoped that Father Goodwin had a believable explanation.

All such thoughts fled from his mind when he went through the door.

The four monks were kneeling before Devine with their hands on their heads.

Devine was stalking up and down before them.

'Talk!' he roared. His demand reverberated through the chapel as he raised a hand ready to slap the nearest monk.

'Stop, Devine,' Nimrod said, walking down the aisle.

Devine cast him a casual glance, then backhanded the monk's cheek, knocking him onto his side. Then he punched the second monk squarely on the nose, making blood fly and rolling him onto his back.

He kicked the third monk in the stomach, making him fold over, then dragged the fourth, Father Goodwin, to his feet and stood with his fist drawn back ready to punch him.

Goodwin looked at him with a calm and defiant smile on his face as if he welcomed the chance to prove he wouldn't fight back.

'Nobody tells me to stop,' Devine muttered.

He waited until Nimrod reached him, then punched Goodwin in the stomach. When Goodwin jerked forward, he delivered a second blow to his chin that sent him tumbling to the floor.

Devine swung round to stand astride his fallen form, facing Nimrod, his fists bunched and his stern gaze boring into him. Nimrod stood between Devine and the three fallen monks.

'Cornelius isn't here,' he said levelly, 'but some people have been staying in one of the buildings.'

Nimrod expected that this news would please Devine, but the marshal scowled.

'I know. You wasted your time, Pinkerton man.'

'So who was here?'

'I was finding that out. Obliged you reminded me.'

Devine stepped to the side and reached down to grab the front of Goodwin's robe.

'Answer the Pinkerton man,' he muttered, hoisting Goodwin to his feet.

'This is difficult for me to — '

Goodwin began before a backhanded slap rocked his head to the side.

'Something happened here,' Nimrod said, moving forward with a hand raised, 'but this isn't the way to find out what it was.'

Devine looked at him with an unconcerned expression, then slapped Goodwin's cheek, knocking him in the opposite direction. This time he released him and let him fall to the floor.

'For once, Pinkerton man, you're right. I'm not getting answers this way.' Devine drew his gun and paced down the line of men until he stood over the monk with the bloodied nose. He aimed the Peacemaker at his chest, but when the monk returned only a benign expression, he aimed it lower at his right knee. 'Who you been hiding?'

'Don't, Devine,' Nimrod said.

'You can die from a leg wound,' Devine muttered, ignoring him, 'but not before I shatter your other leg. So talk before I see how much lead you can take.'

Goodwin caught the targeted monk's eye and opened his mouth, looking as if he'd relent and explain what they'd been doing, but then he shook his head.

'Please stop,' he murmured. 'This situation isn't what it seems.'

That plea was enough for Nimrod. He slipped backwards for a half pace and reached for his gun. But his hand had yet to touch leather when with alarming speed Devine turned at the hip, his gun arcing round to aim at his chest.

'So the Pinkerton man's got guts,' Devine said with relish. 'Nobody threatens me and lives.'

'Until today,' Nimrod said, still moving his hand slowly towards his gun.

Devine firmed his gun hand and gave a grim smile.

'Worst last words I've ever heard.'

Devine paced up to him. Having no doubt that he would shoot, Nimrod slapped a hand to his holster. He drew and then swung his gun up, but with a move like lightning Devine jerked forward and clubbed him about the temple with his Peacemaker.

Nimrod teetered. The chapel seemed to swirl around him. Somewhere a bell tolled steadily. His gun fell from his slack fingers, the clatter it made on the floor echoing so loudly it made his head rattle.

Unable to keep upright, he fell to his knees and keeled over onto his chest. He sensed that Devine was standing over him, but he couldn't summon the strength to move. His vision darkened.

Light returned and then faded. Screams invaded his mind. The reek of burning flesh filled his nostrils and he fought to crawl away from the smell, but his mind told him that he was moving only in a dream.

That dream became more troubling when he crawled closer to a row of cowering monks. They were pleading for mercy.

Standing over them and revelling in their torment was the impossibly huge figure of Marshal Devine. He was whistling contentedly. Flames surrounded them all.

'Hell,' Nimrod murmured. Through sheer force of willpower, he struggled his way back to consciousness to escape his bizarre vision of a hell on earth.

When he opened his eyes, he found that he'd been stood upright. As he couldn't move, he looked down. He gulped.

He was now awake, and he was still in hell.

8

'I've caught Cornelius Lee,' Sheridan Cox said, leaning forward in the saddle.

'Where is he?' Mayor Halloway asked before he cast a pointed look behind Sheridan at the Devil's Hump.

While Halloway ran his gaze over the arc of boulders that spread out around them, confirming that Sheridan had come alone, Sheridan considered the two men who had accompanied the mayor.

It appeared that the trip out of town had given him an opportunity to use his two recently hired guns. Sheridan drew their attention to a high spot amidst the boulders.

'Mason and Nash are guarding him until I hand him over to your hired guns.'

'When Cornelius has been handed over to justice,' Halloway said, his voice harsh as he didn't try to disguise his irritation at these strained pleasantries, 'I won't need their protection.'

Sheridan rubbed his hands, presenting a show of being pleased.

'And you can have him, but I have a small amendment to our deal.' Sheridan lowered his voice. 'Pay me half the money now and the other half when I hand him over.'

'No deal.' Halloway's flicked glance made his two hired guns edge their horses forward.

'You'll deal. You want Cornelius alive and if I don't return within five minutes, my associates will kill him.'

'Then kill him. I had wanted to see the defeat in his eyes, but his dead body will suffice.'

The two men locked gazes. Sheridan was the first to look away.

Sheridan took a deep breath and ground his jaw to give the impression he was giving the matter careful and troubled consideration. Then he gave a brief nod, making the two hired guns snort with disgust, suggesting they'd not expected this confrontation to peter out so tamely.

'I'll bring him here two hours before sundown,' Sheridan said with a defeated air. He backed his horse away.

'And you can rest assured that I'll have the money,' Halloway said with a gleam in his eye. The hired guns backed up the possibility of his being duplicitous with wide smirks.

Sheridan continued to back away until with a sharp gesture he tore the reins to the side and turned his horse. He headed off to the boulders, and by the time he'd reached the Devil's Hump he was hurtling along at a gallop. Although he didn't look back, the three men's gazes bored into his back.

After he'd crested a rise he drew to a halt and stood looking straight ahead. Presently a low whistle sounded from a high boulder. He waited for another minute and a longer whistle sounded.

Sheridan dismounted. With a brief

glance over his shoulder to confirm he hadn't been followed, he clambered up to that boulder, emerging at a point where he could look down at the scene of the failed negotiation.

The mayor and his men were riding towards Bigelow Town and showing no sign that they would turn back. Sheridan still watched them until the terrain took them out of his view. Only then did his colleague Mason shuffle along to join him.

'Halloway didn't notice the other men hiding out there,' Mason said.

'Don't get too confident and keep looking out for trouble,' Sheridan replied, with his gaze still set on the plains. 'Halloway is a slippery snake.'

'Sure,' Mason said. He turned to climb up to a higher point, leaving Sheridan to slip down the slope on the opposite side to town.

Sheridan negotiated a thin gap between two boulders that had rolled down the slope and then lodged against each other. He came out in an enclosed space that was hidden from sight in all directions.

Two men were sitting in this effective hideaway: his other colleague, Nash, and the subject of the negotiations, Cornelius. Both men were leaning back against opposing boulders.

'Any problems?' Nash asked.

'Nope,' Sheridan said. He sat in the centre of the space with the two men on either side. 'Halloway was arrogant, so I lulled him into a false sense of security by letting him beat me in our negotiations.'

'It's always wise to play to his strengths,' Cornelius said with a chuckle. He contemplated Sheridan and then lowered his voice. 'But will you want to win our negotiations?'

Sheridan narrowed his eyes. 'We agreed to split what we can get from him fifty-fifty.'

Cornelius stood up and stretched. Then, with a determined slap of a fist against a thigh, he removed his six-shooter from his holster and threw it to Sheridan.

‘That’s the deal you wanted, but I’m the prisoner.’ Cornelius spread his hands to show he was now unarmed and vulnerable. ‘I’m taking all the risks. Seventy-five-twenty-five is more to my liking.’

Sheridan hefted the gun and then aimed at a high spot above their heads with one eye closed in a mime of being careful with his aim.

‘I’m sure it is, but if I agree, you’ll have to hope that worrying about our deal doesn’t affect my aim.’

Cornelius went over to Sheridan and, using a single finger, he pointed the barrel downwards before he looked him in the eye.

‘You’re bounty hunters. We’re not. We need the money for something that’s more important than women, liquor and gambling.’

‘Fifty-fifty.’ Sheridan strained to raise the gun higher. ‘Or nobody gets what they want.’

‘Except I haven’t yet started on Mayor Halloway. He’s now ripe for the picking. There's more money to be made here than just this deal.'

Sheridan lowered his head slightly, so Cornelius removed his finger, letting the gun swing upwards.

Then they both smiled.

* * *

Nimrod tried to move forward, but when a solid band tightened around his neck he jerked to a halt. He twisted and confirmed that a noose constrained him. Then he ran his gaze upwards to see that he'd been secured to an upright cross.

He struggled, but his hands had been tied together behind his back and his legs were bound. Having understood his situation, he then steeled himself to check on the state of the monks.

It was as bad as he had feared.

They were all dead. That observation made Nimrod look around the chapel, but if Devine was still around, he wasn't in here.

Nimrod flexed his back, putting his mind to the task of freeing himself, but he had leeway of only a few inches. He scraped his feet from side to side searching for purchase.

He found none on the smooth floor, but the noise he made was answered with a gurgling sound. He looked from one monk to the next, wondering which one had survived to make the noise.

The monk he had tried to help lay still, his form bloodied from repeated gunshots. A gunshot to the back of the head had dispatched the second monk, while the third monk had clearly tried to run away, as he lay in the aisle with a gunshot wound bloodying his back.

Father Goodwin was the one who had survived. He sat propped up against the altar, his head bowed and his hands cradling his bloodstained stomach.

'Father,' Nimrod croaked. He cleared his throat and tried again. 'Father Goodwin.'

Goodwin stayed looking down, but

the gurgling noise sounded again, at least proving he was still alive. A thin stream of blood dripped from his mouth into his lap and, with a shake of the head, he cleared his mouth and then looked up. Tortured, staring eyes met Nimrod's.

'He's gone,' Goodwin whispered.

'I'm sorry,' Nimrod said. 'I tried to stop him.'

'I know, but don't worry. On the final day he'll be judged.'

'I'd prefer to see him judged in this life.'

'I understand your anger, but put your hate aside lest you too be judged and found wanting by the only judge that matters.'

Nimrod managed a thin smile. 'We can discuss this all day and not persuade the other to change their opinion. So for now we need to help each other.'

Nimrod ran his gaze up the rope that secured him to the cross and back down again. With his strength returning as he shook off his dazed feeling, he reckoned he might be able to topple the cross and free himself, but he would prefer to avoid committing more desecration.

'I don't reckon,' Goodwin said, 'I have the strength to stand up and free you.'

Goodwin glanced down at his robes and the movement of his hands revealed a gleaming object. Devine had left a knife buried deep in his guts.

Nimrod winced. 'He was determined to get answers.'

'He was, and so were you.' Goodwin gave a wan smile. 'But you haven't sought them.'

Nimrod shrugged, figuring that Goodwin knew he would die soon and only he could decide whether he wanted to unburden himself.

'Know this: I intend to deliver justice and I'm a fair man.'

'Cornelius Lee did stay here,' Goodwin said. His voice was low and barely audible, but it gained strength once he'd started speaking. 'But his activities aren't what they seem. He's not an outlaw, just someone who needed guidance and moral support.'

'I'm pleased he sought your help after he'd killed Yorath Halloway.' Nimrod sighed when Goodwin shook his head. 'But the most important thing is what happens now. You have to trust me to deal with Cornelius fairly. So where did he go?'

'I don't know.'

'Then what did you tell Devine to stop him killing you? And me for that matter?'

'I don't know that either. He tied you up first, so perhaps he wanted you left alive to bear witness.' Goodwin looked aloft as he considered. 'Then something I said satisfied him and he left.'

Nimrod waited for more details, but when Goodwin didn't provide them he shook himself, reminding the monk of his predicament.

'We'll talk about this when I'm free.' Nimrod glanced at his bonds. 'That knife has to come out and, if you can summon up the strength to use it to cut through my bonds, I can stop you bleeding to death.'

Goodwin shook his head. 'My hands are all that's stopping my guts spilling out on to the floor. Nothing you can do will save me. But I can choose the moment I die.'

He straightened his back and then rolled forward on to his knees. A spasm contorted his body and bright fresh blood flowed over his hands.

Hurriedly he got to his feet, as if he doubted he would live to try again, and stood bowed. Then, still doubled over, he stepped towards Nimrod until he walked into him.

Nimrod could do nothing to help him other than to murmur encouragement. So, while propping himself up against him, Goodwin worked his way around his body until he was leaning against the cross. This took him out of Nimrod's eyeline, although he could hear the monk's ragged breathing.

'What now?' Nimrod whispered.

Coldness pressed against the backs of Nimrod's hands. Only when he tried to move them aside did he realize that he'd felt the hilt of the knife in Goodwin's belly.

'Now it's my turn to receive judgment for my actions,' Goodwin said. 'This is the only way. Draw straight and true.'

With his hands constrained, the requested action was perhaps beyond him, but Goodwin was murmuring in pain, suggesting he couldn't stay upright for long, so Nimrod did as ordered. He twisted his hands to secure a grip of the hilt.

Goodwin sighed, partly from the pain, but perhaps also in relief as the end of his torment approached. For his part Nimrod rehearsed the motion in his mind.

'Prepare yourself,' he said, using a soft tone.

'Just keep a firm grip,' Goodwin whispered. 'And bless you.'

Goodwin fell away from him.

From the corner of his eye and with his neck strained, Nimrod saw the monk land on the floor. He'd fallen with his body held stiffly, showing that he hadn't stumbled. He had pushed himself away to leave the knife in Nimrod's hand.

Nimrod wasted no time in turning the knife in his grip. He sawed through the taut rope around his wrist. Then he reached up to tear away the noose at his throat.

A few moments later the rope around his ankles was gone and he was kneeling beside Goodwin, but he was too late.

Blood was still oozing out from his belly, but it did so with a weak flow. Nimrod poked around the wound, seeking a way to help him, but he got no reaction.

Goodwin was no longer breathing.

With a heavy heart Nimrod checked on the other monks. Thankfully, for them there was nothing he could do, so he pocketed the knife.

As he'd done at the other mission, he dragged the bodies outside and then found blankets to wrap them up in. The ground was hard, but he still searched until he found an area that had been used to grow vegetables.

He selected a corner facing the chapel and then buried the bodies in a long trench. He then constructed a crude cross from two planks and set it on the mound of earth.

When he'd finished, the sun was high in the sky. So he sat in the shade from the chapel and contemplated the monks' grave.

He failed to gather any new ideas as to where he could go next in search of Cornelius and Devine, so he went inside. He sat on the front pew where he forced himself to recall the last events he could remember before Devine had knocked him out.

'You worked out where Cornelius had gone,' he said to himself, 'but how?'

He again looked around the chapel,

but he saw no clues and had to admit that for all his sadistic cruelty Devine was a shrewd man who had somehow always been one step ahead of him. And despite having spent no time with Cornelius, the marshal appeared to have deduced more about his movements and plans than he had.

He moved to rise and his hand brushed a pile of well-thumbed Bibles stacked on the pew beside him. He was sure they'd all been piled up when they'd arrived, but one book had been set aside. It lay on its front with the pages splayed, as if it had been discarded.

He picked up the Bible and quickly read the chapters on the displayed pages. They didn't appear relevant, so he flicked through the book.

Spots of blood marred several pages and other pages were ripped as if the previous reader had riffled through them quickly. As that reader had probably been Devine and, as Nimrod didn't reckon he was a man who sought inspiration in the Bible, he scanned the pages where the blood had soaked through.

He found nothing of interest and was about to put the book down when his casual thumbing brought him to the first page.

In the top corner were the initials *CL* followed by the number, presumably a date: '69.

'Cornelius Lee,' Nimrod murmured, standing up, his thoughts whirling as he picked up on the detail that must have intrigued Devine.

He stood and paced back and forth. The mission had seen better days and he knew that once, many years ago, it had cared for orphans. Cornelius could have been one of those orphans and that was why he had come here and why the monks had been prepared to hide him away.

He returned to the Bibles and sifted through them. They were old, not all of them retained initials that identified their original owners, and some initials had been scribbled down when later generations had made their mark. But he found a GW with the same date, suggesting that Gilchrist Wheaton, Cornelius's closest adviser and oldest friend, might have been an orphan here too.

The last Bible he opened provided a final intriguing clue that tied in with what Jerome Malleson had said before he died in Lone Star. The initials were *TH* and the date was the same as the other two, signifying that another orphan had been Thomas Halloway, Bigelow Town's mayor and Cornelius Lee's nemesis.

'You all lived here as children,' Nimrod said, putting the Bible down, 'and yet the monks sided with Cornelius and not with the most powerful man in the county.'

With that bemusing revelation spurring him on, he left the chapel.

When he reached his horse the dull sheen of gun-metal on a nearby post caught his attention. Nimrod approached and he found that Devine had left his Peacemaker and holster dangling there for him to collect.

'Nobody threatens you and lives,' Nimrod said, strapping on the holster, 'so why didn't you kill me?'

9

Mayor Halloway was approaching and he was on time, as Sheridan Cox had expected him to be. The mayor always fulfilled his easy commitments.

Flanking him were his two hired guns. For his part Sheridan apparently had only his two colleagues Mason and Nash, who were riding alongside Cornelius. But he had chosen a spot close to the Devil's Hump and, unlike earlier when they'd made their deal in the outcropping of boulders, Cornelius's men had holed up.

He had arranged for the meeting to be at the limit of their firing range to give the impression that Halloway would have nothing to worry about. To bolster that impression Sheridan moved forward to meet Halloway a few dozen yards on from the other three.

On the way he glanced over his

shoulder and gave a nod of encouragement. Cornelius's only response was to lower his head and assume an appropriately defeated air.

'I'm pleased you're on time,' Sheridan called out, maintaining the impression that he was eager to please and yet was nervous of duplicity.

'And you've brought Cornelius,' Halloway said, drawing to a halt.

Halloway looked past Sheridan to consider Cornelius and then the men with him. His gaze took in the outcrop behind them and the surroundings before it ended with a consideration of his two hired guns.

Sheridan had no doubt he was weighing up the possibility of holding out, so he was relieved when Halloway gathered up a saddle-bag. He underhanded the bag towards him, but he did so weakly, and the bag thudded into the ground ten feet short of Sheridan's horse.

'I'll fulfil my part of the bargain,' Sheridan said, moving to dismount, 'when I've counted the money.'

'While you count it,' Halloway urged. His hired guns backed up his command by edging forward with their hands close to their holsters.

'All right,' Sheridan said. 'We do this deal one step at a time.'

Sheridan gestured and Nash urged Cornelius to move on. When their prisoner complied, Sheridan dismounted and headed to the saddlebag. He knelt beside the bag. As he flipped it open, Halloway's hired guns spread out.

One rider moved backwards so that he could keep everyone in view. The other man moved on to take control of Cornelius. Nash herded him on so that the exchange would take place ten yards to Sheridan's left.

For this subterfuge to work and, for them to get away with the money while Cornelius remained free, they needed good timing.

With that in mind, Sheridan sought to confirm quickly that the risk was worth taking. It was likely that Halloway had tried a subterfuge of his own, but when Sheridan riffled through the bag, the wads of bills appeared thick enough to provide the requested payment.

Sheridan picked a wad at random and flicked through it, confirming that the bills were genuine and not just cut paper.

'The money's there,' Halloway called. 'I want to end this today.'

Even though he didn't believe him, Sheridan nodded and closed the saddlebag. He looped the bag over a shoulder and stood, but he didn't return to his horse. He would do that in around a minute when . . .

A distant gunshot pealed out followed by two more.

The shooting had been from the outcrop, as arranged, but the peals had come earlier than planned. Worse, the sounds had been muffled and none of the gunfire had kicked dirt anywhere near them.

Without difficulty Sheridan registered surprise with an open mouth before he swirled round to look at the Devil's Hump.

Another shot sounded and two men appeared briefly on the top of a high boulder. A large man was hurrying after one of Cornelius's men.

A gunshot blasted and the pursued man pressed a hand to his back as he toppled over. He tumbled to the ground and landed in an explosion of dust. The large man then moved away in search of more targets.

'Double-crossed,' Sheridan muttered as gunfire rattled on.

'By you!' Halloway shouted.

Sheridan swirled round to face Halloway and, if the mayor was lying, he was doing it convincingly. He and his two hired guns were glaring up at the outcrop with wide-eyed shock and perhaps even fear.

Sheridan got confirmation of what was happening when Nash cried out in pain and, while clutching his side, he tumbled from his horse.

The hired gun nearest to him moved forward to secure Cornelius, who scrambled for the pistol he'd hidden away in his jacket. Judging that he could take care of himself, Sheridan clutched hold of the saddlebag and faced Halloway, but the mayor had already drawn his gun.

Ill-directed gunfire splayed around Sheridan's feet and, with the mayor's horse rearing and making him a difficult target, he beat a hasty retreat to his horse.

Sporadic gunfire resounded on the outcrop and gunshots exploded behind him as Mason and the other hired gun traded gunfire.

By the time Sheridan mounted his horse, the situation had turned disastrous. Mason had been shot. He slipped from his horse and landed in a lifeless heap on the ground while Cornelius thrust his hands high. One of Halloway's hired guns directed him to drop his pistol.

Sheridan swirled his gun round towards the other hired gun, but that man had already aimed his gun at him. Sheridan stilled his hand.

'What's your plan here?' he demanded, looking at Halloway.

'Are you still claiming,' Halloway said, pointing at the Devil's Hump where everything had now gone ominously quiet, 'that you know nothing about this ambush?'

'This wasn't my doing.'

Halloway glared at him, but then he shook his head.

'I don't care what you were trying to achieve. I have Cornelius and you have the money. Attempt anything now and you'll die.'

He gestured for the hired gun to fetch the prisoner. Cornelius shot Sheridan a bemused look, and Sheridan shrugged. Then Cornelius turned away before Halloway noticed their silent communication.

When Cornelius reached the group Halloway swung his horse around and the hired guns flanked Cornelius. One man levelled a gun on their prisoner and the other turned in the saddle to keep a gun on Sheridan.

Sheridan reckoned he didn't have an option other than to stay put. He waited until they were a hundred yards away.

'I guess,' he said to himself as he watched the group ride away, 'that I'll be getting more than fifty per cent, after all.'

Then he turned to face the outcrop where all was still. He hurried on, taking the route he'd used after his earlier meeting with Halloway.

At the back of the outcrop he considered the boulders and the positions where Cornelius's men should have been, but he saw none of them and neither did he see any movement.

He swung the saddlebag round to rest it against his back, then clambered up to the place where he and Cornelius had holed up between two large boulders. Nobody was there, so he climbed up to where Wallace, one of Cornelius's most trusted men, had been positioned.

Wallace was lying on his chest with his back holed several times. Sheridan was moving to turn the body over when a long shadow spread out beside him. A tuneless whistle sounded.

He turned to see that the formidable form of Marshal Devine was standing before the low sun.

The lawman narrowed his eyes with menace making Sheridan wince and then duck away. A gunshot kicked shards from the rock to his side.

With his head down he headed for cover. Then he hurried on to a steep slope that would let him reach the high point on the outcrop. Using hands and feet he scurried upwards, but before he crested the topmost boulder a warning cry sounded above.

'That's far enough!'

The voice was shaking, but Sheridan recognized the speaker.

'Gilchrist,' he said, 'it's me.'

He raised his head over the edge of the boulder and Gilchrist Wheaton came into view. He was lying on his chest with his gun aimed down at him, clearly having got into a position where he could shoot anyone who tried to reach him.

'You were lucky I didn't shoot,' Gilchrist murmured. He shuffled backwards to give Sheridan room to join him. 'I thought you were Marshal Devine coming back to finish me off.'

Sheridan rolled onto the top to face Gilchrist.

'How many did he leave?'

Gilchrist didn't reply for a while, his manic, darting eyes providing their own full account of the battle that had raged.

'You, me,' he whispered. 'That's all that — '

A horrified look overcame Gilchrist's face before he scrambled away on his hands and knees. Within seconds he'd slipped over the edge of the boulder and disappeared from view down the other side.

Sheridan heard grit move behind him and the same tuneless whistle as before sounded. He jerked to the left, his quick movement saving him from a bullet that would have sliced into his back.

He rolled over twice, then slid over the edge after Gilchrist. He came to rest with his chest pressed to the rock and only his face peering over the top of the boulder.

As he'd feared, Devine had followed him up the slope, his movements having been impressively silent for such a large man.

Devine considered him with contempt. Then he stopped whistling. He jerked his gun to the side to pick him out.

Sheridan was an accurate shot, but he wasn't fast with his aim, so he moved his feet to the side to let gravity save him. Even so, Devine's gunshot sliced slithers of rock into his right cheek as he slipped down the boulder, taking the marshal from his view quickly.

He slid for around fifteen feet until he crunched down on to a ledge, sending a jarring pain shooting up his legs. As his calves and ankles were throbbing, he had to sit down and rub feeling back into his muscles before he could move off.

While he flexed his legs he looked around for Gilchrist, but he'd already gone to ground. So feeling heartened Sheridan followed his lead.

With his gun held low he set off around the boulder, hobbling for the first few steps until desperation let him run off the pain. He rounded the boulder and then came to a skidding halt.

Devine was standing before him with his feet planted wide apart, his gun held across his chest and pressed to his shoulder.

'So you're Marshal Devine,' Sheridan said, unable to hide the awe in his tone at the speed and silence with which he must have moved.

'So you're the skunk,' Devine grunted, 'who was trying to double-cross Mayor Halloway.'

'I was, but you sided with the wrong man, Devine.'

'I side with nobody.' Devine took a long pace forward.

'What do you want with me?' Sheridan murmured, backing away for a pace. 'I'm a bounty hunter.'

'The only people worse than outlaws and Pinkerton men.' Devine snorted, his gun hand twitching. 'Now, bounty man, drop your gun and give me the money. As a reward I'll kill you quickly.'

Sheridan glanced at his gun, mentally rehearsing the motion of swinging it up to aim at the marshal.

'In that case . . . '

Sheridan used his free hand to lift the saddlebag from his shoulder and hold it at arm's length. He swung the bag back and forth in preparation of launching it towards Devine's feet.

On the third swing he met Devine's cold gaze. Then he released the bag and jerked the gun up.

Two gunshots roared.

10

The gunfire had died out, but Nimrod still approached the Devil's Hump carefully.

He had been returning to Bigelow Town to follow the same hunch that he reckoned Devine had followed: that, as Cornelius Lee and Mayor Halloway were connected in ways that weren't commonly known, Cornelius wouldn't stray far from town. He hadn't expected to find evidence that his hunch was correct so quickly.

He drew up before the outcrop and his gaze alighted on a body lying sprawled on the ground. He rode around it and, from the saddle, he was able to confirm that it was Eddie, one of Cornelius's gang.

Eddie had been shot in the back and his broken limbs suggested he had tumbled down the rocks from a high point. When Nimrod followed the passage Eddie must have taken, he saw another body lying trapped between two rocks halfway down.

For the next thirty minutes he searched around. More shot men were around the rocks and, further away from the outcrop, he found the bodies of the two bounty hunters who had been with Sheridan Cox in Mayor Halloway's office.

When he'd completed his search, he had accounted for everyone other than Gilchrist Wheaton, Sheridan Cox, and Cornelius himself.

That left the question of who had wiped them out, so he stood back, picturing the scene.

Sheridan's group had tracked down Cornelius Lee, he presumed. A gunfight had ensued and only two out of the three of Cornelius, Sheridan and Gilchrist had survived.

He looked up at the body lying halfway down the outcrop, but no matter from which angle he looked at it he couldn't tell who it was. He sought out various ways up, but in the end he had to clamber to the top and work his way down.

He was ten feet above the body when he saw a hand move as the man tried to raise the gun that he was still clutching. Nimrod stopped.

'It's me, Nimrod Dunn,' he called. 'I only want to help you, but if you don't lower that gun, I'll leave you there to rot.'

The man stopped trying to move the gun. Instead, he raised his head to let Nimrod see that the survivor was Sheridan Cox.

His smile, the one feature that Nimrod remembered most about him, had been replaced with a pained grimace which, as Nimrod got closer, he saw came as a result of a gunshot wound. His chest was bloodied and he didn't have the strength to extricate himself from the rocks that had trapped him on either side.

It took Nimrod ten minutes to free him, as every manoeuvre he tried made

Sheridan mutter in pain. In the end he had to ignore his complaints and just tug his legs until he dragged his body out of the gap.

He deposited him on a flat rock. Then he sat back to let him gather his breath. After a minute of pained wheezes, Sheridan contemplated him.

'Obliged,' he murmured.

'You should consider yourself lucky after finding Cornelius Lee. This looked like it was a fearsome gunfight.'

'It had nothing to do with Cornelius.' Sheridan took deep breaths. 'This was Marshal Devine's work. He appeared from nowhere. I reckon most died without even knowing who was wiping them out.'

Nimrod looked aloft. 'Everyone?'

'Except for Gilchrist Wheaton. After Devine shot me, he went after him. The last I saw of Gilchrist he was hightailing it away with Devine in pursuit.'

'And Cornelius?'

'That's a long story. I'll tell you about it later.'

Nimrod beckoned Sheridan to raise his hands to let him see the extent of the damage. Blood stained his vest front, the hole being to the side and near his bottom rib.

'It's rare for anyone to survive when Devine's shooting, but if you're to be one of them, we need to get down off this outcrop and get you to help.'

Sheridan winced. 'I was afraid you'd say that.'

The next thirty minutes were difficult for both men.

Nimrod's only option was to help Sheridan clamber up the Devil's Hump to the top, although within a few feet Sheridan became a burden and Nimrod had to carry his full weight.

On reaching the top he'd have liked to give Sheridan and himself a rest, but Sheridan was flitting in and out of consciousness and the barren top provided no cover from the late-afternoon sun. So he helped him down into the shade behind the outcrop.

Going down proved to be easier than

climbing up and the cooling shade helped Sheridan to revive for long enough to keep himself upright while Nimrod directed him. So they carried on until they reached ground level, where they rested.

With his back to the shaded side of a boulder, Sheridan gained enough strength to smile for the first time. After a long gulp of water from Nimrod's supplies, he moved to get up.

Nimrod bade him to stay sitting. 'We'll leave when you've had more water, and that means we have time for you to tell me all.'

Sheridan rubbed his jaw. 'I found Cornelius Lee, so I arranged to hand him over to Mayor Halloway in return for the bounty on his head. The transfer was going well until Marshal Devine arrived and started shooting everyone up.'

'Why did he shoot up your men as well as Cornelius's?'

Sheridan took another sip of water. This time his thoughtful expression suggested he was drinking slowly to give him time to consider his answer.

'We were all behaving suspiciously. I expected treachery from Halloway, and for my part I was looking for a chance to get more money out of him, but Cornelius's men must have followed us here. It didn't do them no good.'

Sheridan's tone had been guarded suggesting there was more to this story than he was prepared to divulge, but for now he decided not to press him.

'What happened to the money?'

Sheridan winced as if he hadn't considered that until now.

'I dropped the saddlebag with the bounty on the top of the outcrop before I tried to shoot Devine, but he fired first and I fell off the rock. I guess falling must have saved me because he wanted the bag.'

Sheridan raised his eyebrows and Nimrod cast his mind back. He had searched the outcrop and, although he hadn't been looking for a saddlebag, he hadn't seen one. Its most likely fate was one he wouldn't have thought possible before his experiences at the missions.

'Devine must have stolen it,' he said.

Sheridan's shoulders hunched as some of the strength he appeared to have summoned up seeped away. While he could still move himself, Nimrod beckoned him to leave.

Sheridan did so unaided; he even managed to mount up one of the spare horses with only a minimum of help from Nimrod, but afterwards he sat slumped in the saddle clutching his ribs. Nimrod led and headed towards town at a fast walking pace, ensuring they got there quickly without putting Sheridan under too much stress.

A half-mile out of town he veered away to a small house beside a creek. Sheridan pushed on to draw alongside. In the thirty minutes since they'd left the outcrop his face had become ashen and bright blood marred his vest.

'I can make it to town,' he said through gritted teeth, his strained voice confirming he was being optimistic.

'It's lucky for you that I always learn about the areas I operate in. I know every building in and around Bigelow Town. Doctor Taylor lives here.'

'Lucky,' Sheridan murmured before he hunched over so far that Nimrod thought he'd fall, but the gentle rocking motion stood him back upright.

Even so Nimrod didn't think he could hold on for much longer, so he hurried on to the house, calling out for help. A white-haired man emerged and took in the scene with an experienced eye before acknowledging him with a quick wave. He walked back into the house, but he left the door open.

Having alerted the doctor, Nimrod turned back to see Sheridan listing badly in the saddle. He dismounted and hurried on to reach him, but before he could get into position Sheridan tumbled heavily and Nimrod could only break his fall.

He lowered him to the ground, where he lay breathing shallowly. Nimrod stood back, wondering which was the best way to get him to the house that would cause him the least distress.

He settled for just getting him there quickly and, with a hand under each armpit, he dragged Sheridan along. Taylor emerged to help him. He took his legs and together they manoeuvred him through the door and then through a main room to a small surgery, where there was a cleared and scrubbed table.

The doctor got to work, cutting away his vest. He didn't ask questions, but Nimrod provided answers anyway.

'I'm a Pinkerton detective,' he said. 'This man is Sheridan Cox, a bounty hunter who was searching for Cornelius Lee, but it looks as if he received more trouble than he gave out.'

'I don't care about anything other than my patient's health.' Taylor glanced up from his work. 'Is this the only injury he has?'

'Yes.'

'Then I don't need to know anything more.' He pointed to the door back to the main room. 'Get yourself a coffee.

And stay out of my way.'

Nimrod accepted Taylor's gruff manner with a nod. Judging that Sheridan was in the best hands, he headed through to the main room where he lit the stove and made himself a coffee.

He would have to go into town to confirm that, with Cornelius being handed over to justice, the openly known aspect of his mission had been completed. But, with sundown still an hour away, he took the opportunity to rest.

He sat and he must have dozed as the next he knew the light level had dropped and Taylor was nudging his hand with a hot coffee mug. Nimrod stretched and took the coffee, enjoying the pungent fumes and letting them bring him to full alertness.

'Sheridan?' he asked.

'He has a chance,' Taylor said, sitting opposite him. 'The bullet went clean in and deflected out, but it made a mess. Even if he doesn't fade away in the next few hours, the wound could still go bad. On the other hand, if he can keep it clean and he rests, he might live to enjoy having a lurid scar.'

Taylor considered him and asked a silent question with a raised eyebrow.

'I need the money I have on me,' Nimrod said, 'but I'll arrange payment when I get to town. While I'm gone, I don't reckon Sheridan will cause trouble. He was in a gunfight out at the Devil's Hump involving Cornelius Lee's men, Mayor Halloway and Marshal Devine.'

'I understand,' Taylor said with a weary tone, as if the last name clarified everything. 'I don't make judgements on my patients' worth, but after stitching them up, I don't look after men who could attract more trouble. You'll have to get Sheridan to town.'

'I'll do that.'

'But tomorrow will suffice. If the agency is paying, he can rest up for a night.'

With that concluding the arrangements they sat quietly.

Presently Taylor moved to light an oil lamp and Nimrod reckoned this was the right moment for him to head to Bigelow Town to find out what had happened to Cornelius. He pointed to the door and Taylor nodded in a distracted way.

Nimrod noted the reason for his lack of interest when he heard hoofbeats outside. Taylor walked to the door and looked out, craning his neck to see who was arriving. A sharp intake of breath sounded.

'Trouble?' Nimrod asked.

'In a way,' Taylor said.

Nimrod hurried to the window and peered outside. Framed against the darkening sky was a large rider.

He was glaring around with a hand close to his holster as if he expected trouble. He dismounted quickly. Then he paced determinedly to the door, moving himself into a patch of light and confirming his identity.

'Marshal Devine,' Nimrod said. He turned to Taylor. 'Don't tell him that

Sheridan is in the surgery.'

'I have no choice,' Taylor said. 'He's sure to look in there.'

A thud sounded in the surgery, making Nimrod smile.

'Then there'll be nothing for him to see. That noise was Sheridan slipping out through the window.'

Taylor whistled through his teeth as Devine stomped to a halt before the door.

'In that case,' he whispered, 'I hope my handiwork lets him enjoy his last few hours.'

* * *

'How much longer are we going to sit here?' Cornelius Lee asked.

Mayor Halloway uttered a contented chuckle, letting Cornelius know he was pleased that he was the one who had broken the silence.

'You know the answer to that,' he said, as if they were continuing their first exchange from earlier in the day.

Cornelius looked around the office.

'You sneaked me up to your office using a back door, sent everyone away for the rest of the day, and since then you and I have sat here enjoying each other's company.' Cornelius rolled his shoulders, testing the ropes that secured him to his chair. They were as constraining as they'd been the last time he'd tried to move. 'Only you can decide when this ends.'

'Except,' Halloway said, sitting back in his chair and relaxing now that they were talking, 'only you can let me end this.'

'You paid ten thousand dollars for me and lost your son; will my answer be worth that price?'

Halloway clenched his jaw before he mustered a tight smile, his tenseness providing his real answer.

'You should never have defied me. Nobody does that. Give me what I want and this will end.'

'And if I don't?'

'You saw the men who brought you

in. They'll do what I tell them to do and they can do plenty while keeping you just alive enough to carry out my bidding afterwards.'

'I can't do your bidding.'

Halloway narrowed his eyes. 'So your promises were lies. I thank you for your honesty, but you won't thank me for the result.'

Cornelius waited until Halloway moved to rise and summon his hired guns before he coughed.

'Sit down. I never lied to you, but I did expect you to double-cross me, so I took out insurance.'

Halloway sneered. 'My son should have been more than enough insurance.'

'And you should have dealt with me fairly instead of putting a bounty on my head and then hiring — '

'Enough!' Halloway snapped. 'We're not here to debate everything that's happened in our lives starting with the day we were children at the mission and you saved me from a beating.'

'If I remember it right, that beating was at the hands of Maddox Kingsley, a brute of a man who has somehow risen even higher than you have. And yet despite that, you repaid my years of loyalty by running me out of town.'

'As I said, we can debate our lives for ever,' Halloway said, his eyes narrowing with anger. 'We both have grievances we can throw at the other and we both have reasons to be indebted to the other. But I'm prepared to put an end to it all and give us both a fresh start. And all you have to do is agree to do one simple thing for me.'

'If you want a fresh start you need to listen to me. I can't do it . . . ' Cornelius leaned forward as far as his bonds would allow. 'But I've always known someone who can.'

Halloway raised an eyebrow. 'So the great Cornelius Lee admits that some things are beyond his capabilities. That makes this an interesting day. So who is this someone who can do what you can't?'

'He's expensive. You'll have to pay him the same sort of money as you had to pay to get me here.'

'I'll do that. Give me the name.'

Cornelius smiled. 'Come closer and I'll tell you.'

Halloway considered him, clearly expecting deception, but Cornelius's bonds were secure, so he came out from behind his desk. He stopped five feet away, leaving Cornelius to look him over as he relished a moment that, despite Halloway's promises, could well be his last.

'I know of only one man who has the necessary skills,' he said. Then he lowered his voice as he revealed the name, forcing Halloway to strain to hear him.

Afterwards, Halloway punched him in the face.

11

'Come in, Marshal,' Doctor Taylor invited, holding the door wide open.

Marshal Devine grunted an acknowledgement and Taylor stood aside to beckon him in, giving Nimrod enough time to stand behind his chair.

This position gave Nimrod a clear view of the room while letting him keep his gun drawn and out of sight until he got his best chance to take on the marshal. To his surprise, when Devine stormed in through the door and saw him he merely snarled with irritation.

'Thought I was following Gilchrist Wheaton,' he said, 'but it's the Pinkerton man.'

'The Pinkerton man,' Nimrod snapped, unable to keep the anger from his tone, 'whom you left for dead at the mission.'

'If I'd wanted you dead, you would be.' Devine rubbed his shaggy beard, freeing a shower of trail dust. 'Like the rest of the scum.'

Nimrod settled the gun in his grip. 'So you considered the monks to be scum?'

'They hid your friend and made my mission harder.'

Nimrod lowered his head to consider his gun, finding that despite his previous commitment Devine had said the one thing that could stop Nimrod from shooting him. Nimrod couldn't bring down a lawman unless he was sure that the mission was complete.

'You're not as formidable as you think you are, Devine,' Nimrod said, looking up. 'Gilchrist Wheaton is still at large, as is the bounty hunter Sheridan Cox. Neither deserved your shooting them up at the Devil's Hump, so I won't lose sleep when they get you.'

Devine shrugged. 'Bounty men are worse than the scum they track down.'

'The same could be said of some lawmen.'

Devine snorted a harsh laugh before

he turned his icy gaze on Doctor Taylor.

'So you patched up Sheridan, did you? Seems you still don't care what kind of snakes you help.'

'Lucky for you that I don't,' Taylor said, meeting his gaze, 'or you'd be long dead.'

Devine paced up to Taylor. He considered him. Then a brief smile split his beard before he slapped a firm hand on his shoulder and walked past him towards Nimrod.

With a quick gesture Devine swung the chair away from him. He gave Nimrod's drawn gun only a brief glance, then slumped down heavily in the chair. He held out a hand.

Taylor went directly to a cupboard and returned with a whiskey bottle and three clean mugs. He poured them all generous measures.

Devine took his mug without comment while considering Nimrod, who found himself standing with a gun in one hand and a mug of whiskey in the other. He holstered the gun.

'Decided not to kill me, then?' Devine said.

'Not until the mission is over.'

Devine laughed loudly before he took a long swig.

'Good. I'll look forward to seeing another Pinkerton man beg for his life.'

'I thought you killed men who threatened you on sight?'

'Sure.' Devine raised his mug in a mocking salute. 'But you're no threat to me, and no use either.'

Nimrod gripped his mug tightly, but when Taylor smiled at, presumably, a private joke, he took the opportunity to lighten his mood and picked another chair to sit on.

'I found out plenty at the mission, except I didn't have to kill anyone to get that information.'

Devine leaned back in his chair. 'What did you learn from your no-account methods?'

'Cornelius Lee and Mayor Thomas Halloway were orphans at the Mission San Miguel. That tied their fates together and now we're witnessing the end to their personal battle.'

Devine grunted and looked at Taylor.

'You want to answer that, or do you still hide behind those ethics?'

'I do,' Taylor said, 'but in this case I don't know the full story. I do know Halloway tolerated Cornelius beyond all reason. No matter how much trouble Cornelius caused, Halloway helped him out until one day he decided he'd had enough. He ran him out of town and since then Cornelius has escalated their feud.'

'You saw what you were supposed to see,' Devine said.

'Possibly, but Maddox Kingsley is coming to town tomorrow to make a speech. I've heard that the lieutenant governor will congratulate the mayor on the progress he's made so far in cleaning up the county. So Halloway is eager to end the situation with Cornelius before Maddox arrives.'

As Devine made no reply Nimrod spoke up.

'Maddox is also coming to announce he's standing for state governor. Maybe everything will come to a head then.'

Devine downed the last of his whiskey and threw the mug onto a table. He folded his arms and rocked his head back on to the chair. Nimrod waited for his response, but after a few grunts as he settled down, rasping snores sounded.

In exasperation Nimrod looked at Taylor, who uttered a quick laugh. Then Taylor knocked back his whiskey and moved over to collect Devine's mug.

'I assume you're staying now?' he asked.

'Yeah,' Nimrod said. 'I need to watch Devine.'

Taylor shook his head. 'Don't let the snoring fool you. Devine is staying to watch you.'

With that worrying comment, Taylor left to tidy up his surgery. As Nimrod had nothing else to occupy his mind, he did as Devine had done and settled down in his chair.

Despite having dealt with his main concern by deciding to wait until the mission had been completed before he dealt with the brutal marshal, sleep refused to come.

For his part Devine didn't appear concerned. He continued to snore deeply in a way Nimrod reckoned he couldn't feign. But Nimrod had no doubt that if he turned a gun on the marshal he wouldn't get to complete his action.

Troublesome thoughts chased around Nimrod's mind until he fell into a fitful sleep, but it must have been a long and deep one as, when he awoke, light was filtering in through the shutters.

Devine wasn't in his chair.

Nimrod checked in the surgery and then went to the door, finding that Devine's big bay was in the small corral. He walked around the outside of the house, but Devine wasn't visible and Taylor had yet to rise.

The only place left to search was Taylor's derelict barn, which was now just a roofless hulk, struggling to stay upright. He paced into the open doorway and looked around, but the place was empty. He was about to turn away when a shadow flitted over the right-hand wall.

He stared at the spot, bemused by the sight as the sun had yet to rise, but then he realized what he'd seen. A man was walking around the side of the barn and he'd seen him through the gaps in the broken planks.

He turned, aiming to intercept him, but instead he almost walked into a second man who had been sneaking up on him from behind.

Having only a moment to react, he threw up an arm in a warding off gesture, while his assailant converted his stealthy movement into a sudden rush. He piled into Nimrod's chest and then pushed him on into the barn wall.

The rickety structure wasn't strong enough to survive the onslaught and, to the sound of cracking timbers, they both tumbled to the ground in a shower of splinters and broken wood.

Nimrod landed on his back. Although several planks cushioned his fall, his opponent landed heavily on him and then bore down on his chest.

Nimrod fought back by grabbing his opponent's wrists and pushing, but they struggled for only a few seconds before their actions made the walls on either side of them collapse. One section fell away while the other half slammed down on the man's back, making him groan in pain and roll to the side.

With a shake of his head Nimrod put the sprawling man from his mind and fought his way out from under the debris. He emerged from the broken wood as the first man appeared, having skirted around the edge of the collapsed barn.

Nimrod didn't recognize the man and this one was more prepared than the other man had been. He'd already drawn his gun and he had turned it on him. He considered the plight of the other assailant with a jaundiced eye, then turned to Nimrod.

'Reach,' he said.

'Who are you?' Nimrod demanded.

'You don't ask the questions. I want Marshal Devine.' The gunman jerked his gun up and fired over Nimrod's shoulder. 'If you don't want the next shot to hole you, get him out here.'

This was sure to be a false promise, but as Nimrod didn't know where Devine was, he nodded to the house and then took a step towards it, seeking to give the impression that he'd acquiesced.

As the second man struggled to extricate himself from the remnants of the fallen wall, the gunman followed while gesturing for Nimrod to carry on.

A gunshot roared. The gunman screeched and then staggered forward with a hand rising to his chest. A second shot to the forehead made him keel over.

When Nimrod looked along the trajectory the gunshots would have taken, all was still. Although he couldn't work out where the shooter was hiding, he was sure that he had to be Devine.

As the second man was still on his knees Nimrod resolved in a sudden decision to capture him alive for questioning.

He leapt at him and caught him around the shoulders. They both went skittering over the fallen wall until they fetched up on the ground kneeling and facing each other.

Nimrod delivered a swinging punch to his opponent's cheek that rocked him on to his back. The disoriented man pushed himself upright slowly to meet Nimrod's backhanded slap that crashed him down on his back again.

Nimrod got up and stood over him as the man fingered his jaw and shook his head, fighting to regain his senses. Calmly Nimrod drew his gun and aimed it down at him.

'The other one's dead,' he said, 'but I'll spare your life if you tell me who sent you and why you're after Devine.'

The man blinked away his stunned

state and his eyes focused on the gun aimed down at him.

'I believe that promise as much as you believed — '

A gunshot thundered and the man's head flinched backwards with blood spraying. Then he toppled over to let Nimrod see that a slug had hit him between the eyes.

Nimrod swirled round to face Marshal Devine, who was striding towards the body of the first gunman to die.

'Obliged you drew the gunfire again, Pinkerton man,' Devine said. 'Keep this up and we'll make a good team.'

'We won't,' Nimrod muttered. 'He was about to tell me why they were looking for you.'

'Not interested,' Devine said as he stomped to a halt beside the first dead man. 'As you know, nobody threatens me and lives.'

'Then how can you ever learn anything?'

With disdain curling his upper lip, Devine kicked the gunman's body in the chest. Then he launched a long splash of spittle on to its face. He stepped over the body and moved on to the second man, where he repeated the action.

'I'm no Pinkerton man,' he said.

With that declaration he turned away. As he walked towards his horse, he whistled tunelessly.

12

Bigelow Town was in the midst of the usual early-morning bustle when Marshal Devine dismounted outside the mayor's office. Devine was still whistling, as if killing two men before sunup was the ideal way to start the day.

With a saddlebag draped over one shoulder, he stormed straight into the building, took the stairs three at a time, and strode heavily down the upstairs corridor to the main office.

Mayor Halloway was sitting at his desk. He looked up with only mild interest in his eyes, suggesting he had expected someone else to come in. Then he did a double-take before staring at Devine for several seconds in open-mouthed surprise.

'So Marshal Jake T. Devine,' he said with a weary tone, 'has returned to my town.'

Devine hurled the saddlebag across the room so that it clattered down onto Halloway's desk and scattered the sheaf of papers he was working on.

'So,' Devine said, 'a worthless snake is still in charge of this cesspit.'

Halloway opened the bag and drew out a handful of money. He raised an eyebrow in surprise.

'I'm obliged you returned my bounty, but you need to learn how to behave in civilized company.' Halloway pointed a firm finger at him. 'With Cornelius dealt with, you no longer have a reason to be in my town.'

Devine considered the finger, his breath snorting through his nostrils.

'You don't give me orders.'

'I don't, but Lieutenant Governor Maddox Kingsley is due here today to — '

'Pollute the townsfolk's ears with his senseless prattle.'

'He's here to do that,' Halloway said, giving a small smile, 'but he's also coming to announce his intention to be the next governor. And where better to do that than by standing beside his oldest friend and biggest supporter? So I don't want a headstrong lawman around, confusing his message of how he'll clean up this county without resorting to senseless violence.'

While Halloway sat back awaiting his response, Devine stomped up to the desk. He slapped his hands on the desk and glared down at the mayor. Then, with a sudden burst of movement, he grabbed the edge of the desk and tipped it up and over.

As the money fluttered in all directions, Halloway scrambled backwards to avoid the rolling desk, but his quick movement made him tip out of his chair. He landed on his back a moment before the desk slammed down on his legs, pinning him to the floor.

Devine clambered over the desk, dragging a pained bleat from Halloway, to stand beside his trapped form.

'You've not seen senseless violence

before,' he muttered. He stamped on the fallen desk, crushing Halloway's legs. 'This morning you sent your two hired guns to shoot up me and my Pinkerton friend. Why?'

Halloway's only reply was a grunt of pain. Devine pressed down again, dragging another pained screech from the mayor's lips. When Halloway's grunts turned to whimpering, Devine leaned on his knee.

He held the pose for several seconds until, with a snort of disgust that suggested he had relented only to get answers in another way, Devine pushed the desk off Halloway's legs. He righted the chair and deposited Halloway on it.

'I . . . I . . . ' Halloway murmured while rubbing his legs and then flexing them to make sure they still worked. 'I told two men to scout around. I don't want any problems when Maddox Kingsley comes and — '

'Wrong answer,' Devine roared. He slapped the sole of his boot against

Halloway's chest and sent him tumbling backwards.

The moment Halloway hit the floor Devine was on him. He hoisted the mayor to his feet, stood him upright, and then thundered a low blow into his stomach that had him folding over and coughing in pain.

Halloway staggered around on the spot, but that only succeeded in placing his back to Devine, giving the marshal the room to kick his rump and send him tumbling into the fallen desk.

Halloway thrust out a hand to stop himself, but he failed. He sprawled over the desk and landed in an undignified heap on the other side.

Devine vaulted the desk and again hoisted Halloway to his feet.

'You have no right to treat me like this,' Halloway murmured, but Devine ignored him and slammed a short-armed jab into his stomach.

Halloway doubled over and heaved. Then he spilled his breakfast over the desk.

Devine waited until he'd stopped heaving, then grabbed the back of his head. He forced him to his knees over the splash of vomit.

'Last chance to explain before I make you lick up every drop.'

Halloway averted his face from the reeking mess and looked up at Devine with pleading eyes. What he saw in Devine's gaze gave him no hope and he started blabbering.

'Cornelius Lee planned to kill Maddox Kingsley.' Halloway cringed, clearly expecting another blow, but Devine gave an encouraging grunt. 'One of his men, Gilchrist Wheaton, survived the bloodbath at the Devil's Hump. So I told those men to find Gilchrist and quash the plot.'

'And that required them to shoot up a US marshal and a Pinkerton man?'

'I also told them to reclaim the bounty money I gave Sheridan Cox.' Halloway sighed. 'If they're still alive, they'll confirm my orders.'

Halloway turned his head away,

resigned to his fate.

Long moments passed until, with an angry grunt, Devine pushed Halloway's face into the pool of vomit and ground it down. Then he turned on his heels and strode away.

* * *

The stage was on time.

Three miles out of Bigelow Town it emerged from a spreading dust cloud, the sun at its back casting shimmering light off the sweat-slicked horses and the amassed weaponry of Maddox Kingsley's flanking guards. He had taken no chances during this rare and fleeting visit to Jackson County.

As the riders bore down on Devine and Nimrod, showing no sign of stopping, Devine leaned towards Nimrod.

'Find Sheridan Cox?' he asked.

'He's gone to ground,' Nimrod shouted over the rumbling of the wheels, summing up quickly his two hours of fruitless searching.

Devine shook his head. 'You Pinkerton men sure do waste time. He'll be with Gilchrist Wheaton now.'

'How can you be sure?'

Devine rubbed his beard and laughed. 'The mayor spilled it all.'

As the horses loomed closer Nimrod judged that even Devine would have to move aside, but instead he remained squarely before the stage, keeping his steed on a tight rein.

The driver hollered for them to move aside while the flanking guards levelled guns on them. Devine's response was merely to glare at them, as if he expected that the force of his gaze alone would make them stop.

Either it worked or the driver caught a glimpse of Devine's star as he slowed the stage and slewed it off the trail. The riders parted, some men looking around for trouble while the rest surrounded Nimrod and Devine. They all kept one hand on the reins while the other rested close to their holsters.

Nimrod and Devine remained silent

as the stage trundled past and came to a halt thirty yards on.

'You men got a death wish?' the nearest rider asked.

Devine turned his steely gaze on him. 'Who dares to threaten a US marshal?' he demanded.

'Nobody's threatening you. We're being careful.'

'We all need to be,' a voice said from behind. 'That's Marshal Devine, still alive and still at large.'

Nimrod turned to see that Maddox Kingsley was leaning out of the stage window. Maddox cast him a narrow-eyed glance which confirmed that his comment had been a reminder that he hadn't forgotten his earlier order.

Devine swung his horse around and barged between two riders to stand before the stage.

'Go to Bigelow Town,' he said, 'and you'll be shot to hell.'

Maddox shrugged. 'I'd be disappointed if nobody tried to kill me, and that's why I've brought these men.'

'You don't need them. You have me and a Pinkerton man.'

'In which case your help is appreciated.' Maddox gestured past Devine to Nimrod. 'He'll travel with me while you'll ride alongside and ensure that my life's not endangered.'

Having stated his case, Devine said nothing more. Five minutes later the stage and accompanying guards resumed their journey to town.

Nimrod sat in the stage opposite Maddox while Maddox's aide, after much grumbling, took his horse. For several minutes Maddox said nothing, keeping his notes for his forthcoming speech on his lap as he contemplated Nimrod and waited for him to explain himself.

'Devine is right,' Nimrod said, having decided that nothing he could say would pacify Maddox. 'A man called Gilchrist Wheaton will try to kill you.'

'He sounds unimportant,' Maddox said. 'He won't give Marshal Devine any trouble.'

'I know, and that's why the marshal remains useful, for now.'

'Except I can't make a speech about cleaning up the county lawfully when a gun-toting marshal is shooting up half the town searching for one man.' Maddox gave a thin smile. 'And yet you still dare to claim that you haven't completed your mission because you're concerned for my safety.'

Nimrod considered trying to explain his feelings since being given this mission. But he doubted it would interest Maddox, so he settled for a simple statement.

'Devine is not an easy man to defeat.'

'He's not. That's why I thought you were the man for the job, a careful man who weighs up the situation, waits for an opportunity, and then strikes.'

'In other words, the opposite of Devine.' Nimrod relaxed when Maddox conceded his opinion with a brief nod. 'Rest assured that I'll do what you asked, but only when the mission is complete. You're in danger and your men can't plug every gap, so right now you need a maverick like Devine who'll find Gilchrist before Gilchrist finds you.'

Nimrod concluded with an understanding smile, which Maddox didn't return.

'I have a report on Devine's latest activities.' Maddox set his cold gaze on Nimrod then rummaged through the folders his aide had left. He opened a folder and scanned down the page inside. 'During his over-zealous questioning, Devine killed all the residents of the Mission Santa Cruz.'

'Just the one reported so far, then,' Nimrod murmured to himself.

Maddox slammed the folder shut and hurled it back on the seat.

'I'll make this simple. I gave you a mission. Complete it before I leave town or I'll tell Mayor Halloway you were the Pinkerton detective who stood by while his son got shot to pieces. Your career will then end and, if the rumours about Halloway are true, so will your life.'

13

'Now that Maddox Kingsley has arrived,' Nimrod said, 'Halloway has sewn the town up tight.'

Devine merely grunted and stayed propped up against the mayor's office wall behind the podium. With Maddox and Halloway being in conference in the office, he was glaring at the crowd that was gathering for Maddox Kingsley's speech. He presented the air of a man who reckoned his presence would be enough to deter a gunman from trying to shoot the politician.

Two of Maddox's protectors had positioned themselves on either side of the office door and behind the podium to watch the crowd. The rest were deployed further afield.

Some men concentrated on watching the townsfolk from a variety of positions. Other men were watching the buildings in case Gilchrist planned to take a shot at Maddox through a window or from a high point behind a false-fronted building.

With all the obvious avenues of attack covered, Nimrod and Devine were left with the task of looking out for the unexpected. As Gilchrist was the one man who had got away from the marshal unharmed, Nimrod reckoned Devine wouldn't stand here waiting for long. But it wasn't until Sheriff Trey Thorndike joined them that for the first time he showed an interest in proceedings.

'You planted that good-for-nothing whiskey hound yet?' Devine asked.

'If you mean Sheriff Bill Lawrence,' Thorndike said, 'then despite your intervention we gave him the dignified burial he deserved.'

'You should have set fire to him. With all that liquor in him, he'd have warmed up the town for a week.'

Devine licked his lips as he waited for Thorndike to get riled, but the new sheriff moved on and stood beside Nimrod.

'Has Cornelius Lee volunteered anything useful yet?' Nimrod asked.

Thorndike frowned. 'I don't know. He's not my prisoner yet. Mayor Halloway is looking after him.'

While this information made Nimrod reel in surprise, Devine grunted an oath and stepped forward to loom over Thorndike.

'What kind of yellow-bellied heap of trash are you? Even Lawrence had the guts to stand up for himself.'

'I have to tread carefully,' Thorndike murmured. 'I've only just been — '

'You're the law. Act like it.'

Thorndike looked away from Devine, unable to meet his gaze. A tense silence dragged on until footfalls within the office made the guards beside the door bustle, providing the sheriff with an excuse to leave.

Thorndike sloped away down the boardwalk, but when Mayor Halloway escorted Maddox Kingsley outside

Devine stormed after him. He clamped a firm hand on Thorndike's shoulder and dragged him back. The guards swung round to confront him, but Devine ignored them and joined the two politicians.

'Your sheriff wants his prisoner,' Devine said.

'This isn't the time to discuss such matters,' Halloway said. He fingered a split lip while shuffling backwards for several paces.

'Shut your mouth and respect the law.'

Devine pushed Thorndike forward so that he slammed into Halloway, who had to grab hold of him to stop them both falling over. When he'd righted himself Halloway bristled with indignation, but Maddox stepped forward.

'Let the lawmen have their prisoner,' he urged while sporting a wide and ingratiating smile, 'and then we can avoid an unseemly scene.'

Halloway's eyes darted from side to side as he clearly weighed up the situation, then he gave a reluctant nod.

'But of course,' he said. He pointed to an upstairs window. 'Cornelius is secured in the room beside my office.'

Devine grabbed hold of the back of Thorndike's jacket and dragged him towards the door, leaving Nimrod with a problem. He edged closer to Maddox.

'Stay here and guard you,' he whispered, 'or stay with Devine?'

'I won't govern your every movement,' Maddox said, his tense tone at odds with the exuberant waves he exchanged with the nearest onlookers. 'Your duty is clear.'

Nimrod nodded. 'And that's to keep your sorry hide alive first and to kill a lawman second.'

'You,' Maddox muttered, his angry tone making his cheery expression falter, 'have spent too much time with Devine.'

* * *

Marshal Devine kicked the office door open. He uttered a contemptuous snort and turned to Sheriff Thorndike.

'What's wrong?' Thorndike asked, looking past him.

Devine grabbed his shoulders and shoved him through the doorway. The action made Thorndike wince and he winced again when he saw what had annoyed Devine.

Cornelius wasn't here, but ropes were bunched around the legs of a chair in the centre of the room, showing that someone had been secured here recently.

'Escaped,' Devine muttered. 'That's what happens when the law fails.'

Devine glared at the chair. He kicked it aside before going to the window to look down.

Thorndike joined him at the window. Outside, the crowd was still gathering and Halloway had yet to mount the podium.

Thorndike turned to consider the scene inside, looking for clues as to where Cornelius might have gone. He saw nothing untoward, so, in a thoughtful mood, he picked up one of the severed ropes.

'He must have had a secreted knife with him.'

Devine gave the rope a brief glance. He sneered and strode off to the door.

'You're more useless than the Pinkerton man,' he muttered before disappearing through the door to head into the mayor's office.

Thorndike looked again at the rope; this time he noticed that it had been sliced through cleanly. Yet a man who was trying to free himself would have struggled.

Thorndike hurried to the mayor's office to find Devine sweeping folders to the floor and upending furniture.

'Someone must have rescued him,' he said. 'So now you have to stop wrecking Halloway's office and find two men.'

'And where should I look, lawman?'

'I've lived in Bigelow Town for years. I know of places where they can go to ground. It'll take a while, so you . . . we have to start searching now.'

Devine kicked a table over and then went to the desk. In the middle sat a single sheet of paper.

From the door Thorndike recognized it as being a lithograph of Halloway's speech. The sight appeared to please Devine, as he limited himself to merely slapping the paper aside in irritation and walking to the door.

'Is there another window?' he asked.

'There's a storeroom above us, but Cornelius wouldn't escape only to hide out . . . '

Thorndike trailed off as Devine barged past him and into the corridor. Devine quickly found a narrow flight of stairs that led upwards and he wasted no time in running up them.

Thorndike stopped at the bottom, where he watched the marshal until he disappeared from view. He expected him to return quickly after which they could begin a systematic search of the town, but instead he heard a crunch as Devine kicked in the storeroom door.

A cry of alarm sounded, not

Devine's, then came another crunch.

Thorndike ran up the stairs to find Devine holding Gilchrist Wheaton pressed up against the storeroom wall with his Peacemaker thrust up under his chin, making him stand on tiptoes.

'Time to suffer, scum,' Devine muttered.

'I freed Cornelius,' Gilchrist said defiantly with his breath coming in short bursts. 'That's all that matters.'

'Wrong. All that matters is pain.' Devine widened his eyes, the pause in his threats letting the sounds of the excited crowd drift up to them. 'They won't be able to hear your screams and, rest assured, you will be screaming.'

'I won't talk, no matter what — '

Gilchrist broke off as Devine's straight-armed jab slammed into his guts and made him try to fold over. But Devine was keeping him held up with his gun hand and the motion only made the gun jab more deeply into Gilchrist's neck. He started coughing.

Devine waited until the coughing had stopped, then drew back his fist, ensuring he held it high enough for Gilchrist to see it.

'Your plan is obvious. Even the Pinkerton man and this no-account lawman figured it out.'

Gilchrist glanced at Thorndike with pleading eyes, but Thorndike wasn't minded to intervene to help a man who had been involved in the death of Sheriff Bill Lawrence.

Gilchrist must have seen the anger in Thorndike's eyes as he slumped down, with all hope of a reprieve gone, a moment before a swinging pile-driver of a punch thudded into his kidneys. This time Devine released his grip and let him double over, whereupon Devine slapped two bunched hands with the added weight of the gun down on the back of his neck. Gilchrist collapsed.

Devine stood over Gilchrist waiting for him to lever himself back to his feet. The moment he put his hands to the floor and groggily raised himself, Devine stamped a heel down on his fingers.

'Talk,' he said.

'I — ' Gilchrist screeched as a sickening snap sounded. 'Stop! I'm trying to talk.'

Another snap sounded as Devine ground his heel down.

'Talk faster.'

'Mayor Halloway won't stop Cornelius killing Maddox Kingsley,' Gilchrist blurted out before he paused to screech in pain. 'He wants him dead!'

Devine grunted with approval. Then he twisted his heel, breaking another finger before he stepped off Gilchrist's hand, giving him enough room to shuffle back to the wall, where he sat cringing and cradling his injured hand. Devine rolled his shoulders and stepped back to consider Thorndike.

'Want to crush the other hand?' he asked, grinning.

'No,' Thorndike said, stepping forward, 'and he's had enough. We need to find Cornelius while keeping an eye on Halloway.'

Devine's eyes flared. 'A no-account lawman doesn't tell me it's enough.'

Thorndike took a deep breath and moved between Devine and the groaning Gilchrist.

'Our duty is to save Maddox Kingsley.'

'And I will,' Devine roared.

With a heavy hand he barged Thorndike aside, knocking him to his knees.

'Don't hurt him again,' Thorndike demanded.

Devine kicked out, hitting Gilchrist's shoulder and tipping him over onto his side. The motion made him release his broken hand and so Devine clamped his boot firmly onto it.

'Welcome to my hell, scum.'

Gilchrist screeched in agony. He begged Devine to release him while batting his leg ineffectually with his free hand, but Devine merely bore down. Interspersed between Gilchrist's sobbing pleas was the crunch of bone.

With a heavy gulp Thorndike raised himself onto one knee and drew his gun. His hand shook, so he kept the gun lowered.

'Release him,' he said with a small voice.

Devine didn't even turn as he rocked his heel back and forth.

'I've told you everything,' Gilchrist whined as another crunch sounded. 'I don't know where Cornelius is.'

'Don't care about him. I want the truth.'

'Devine!' Thorndike shouted. 'Enough!'

Devine ignored him. Thorndike got to his feet and moved to the side to stand in Devine's eyeline, but neither he nor Gilchrist noticed him.

'The truth,' Gilchrist whimpered. 'The truth is you don't want Cornelius. Halloway's man is now Sheridan Cox.'

'Go on,' Devine urged, raising his foot from Gilchrist's hand.

Gilchrist snuffled. He used his uninjured hand to raise his bloodied and twisted wreck of a hand and slip it under his jacket for protection. He blurted out his story in a rush.

'Mayor Halloway wanted Cornelius Lee to kill Maddox Kingsley. Cornelius agreed, but he had started helping the old mission that looked after us when we were children. He wanted to rebuild the mission, and that needed a lot of money. Halloway wouldn't meet his price. Then he ran him out of town. Even when Cornelius kidnapped his son, Halloway wouldn't settle.'

'The rest,' Devine said when Gilchrist paused for breath.

'The thing is, Cornelius didn't have the ability to shoot Maddox from a distance. It needed a sharp-shooter and Cornelius knew the best man for the job was Sheridan Cox. So Sheridan and Cornelius have been working together to make Halloway pay a fair price.'

'But why,' Thorndike asked, Gilchrist's outburst making him step forward, 'would Halloway want to kill

Maddox Kingsley? He's his biggest supporter.'

'Maddox's speech will confirm that,' Gilchrist whimpered. 'So when Sheridan shoots him up, Halloway can claim that Maddox would have wanted him to stand for governor in his place. Maddox's supporters will back him.'

Devine leaned down to glare at Gilchrist and favoured him with a grin. Then he swung his gun up and pistol-whipped the side of his head.

Gilchrist collapsed without a sound. Devine turned on his heels. He considered Thorndike's drawn gun.

'At long last,' he said, walking past him, 'you're ready to take on the scum.'

14

'That explains everything,' Nimrod said when Thorndike had finished his breathless account of events back in the mayor's office.

Thorndike leaned back against the office wall and rubbed at his face with a shaking hand. Then he stared at the hand with shock, presumably noting his inability to control his own body.

'Devine will get answers,' he murmured, 'if anyone's left alive to provide them.'

Mayor Halloway was starting his speech to the sprawling crowd that filled the road. His voice was barely audible. Thorndike moved to slope away, his shoulders hunched and his gait uncertain, suggesting he wouldn't be joining in the search.

'Forget the way Devine got his answers from Gilchrist,' Nimrod called after him. 'We need to act on the information.'

'Then you're as bad as Devine is,' Thorndike said. He stopped to glare at Nimrod before he moved off down the road towards the law office.

Nimrod watched him go. He'd heard that Thorndike had been a competent deputy sheriff, but clearly he'd now been appointed to a position that was beyond his abilities. He shook his head and took stock of the situation.

Devine would pursue his usual methods to track down Sheridan Cox, but, Nimrod reckoned, this task required measured consideration.

If Sheridan were a sharpshooter, as Gilchrist had claimed, he would be able to kill Maddox from a distance. He wasn't a fast draw though and he would need time to aim. As he was injured, he would be less mobile and he wouldn't want the gathered people to jostle him.

The assassin would therefore be indoors.

Nimrod ran his gaze along the windows of the buildings opposite, putting himself into the mind of a sharpshooter and thinking through where he'd go. As he appraised the scene, consternation erupted amidst the crowd, breaking his concentration.

Devine was barging through the crowd, aiming for the buildings opposite. One of Maddox's guards was hurrying after him.

Despite the people crowded before him, Devine built up a strong pace and he reached the boardwalk opposite ten yards ahead of his pursuer. He grabbed a man standing outside the mercantile and pointed. This man let him into the store.

When the marshal had disappeared from view Nimrod returned to considering the buildings. Devine would follow the simple policy of exploring every building until he found Sheridan, but he was concentrating on the opposite side of the road, leaving Nimrod to explore this side.

Nimrod looked for likely buildings where Sheridan might hole up and his thoughts returned to the injury the bounty hunter had suffered. That would limit his mobility, so he would already be in position and he would have needed comfortable surroundings while he waited.

Nimrod slapped a hand against his thigh in triumph and made his way around the back of the podium, through the massed guards.

A loud cheer sounded and Halloway waved for the applauding crowd to quieten after making, presumably, a popular point. He was in good spirits as he delivered his speech and, unnoticed, Nimrod slipped by into clear space on the boardwalk.

The First Chance saloon was three buildings along from the mayor's office, and he could reach it while staying on the boardwalk beneath the canopy.

If his hunch were right, the podium would be visible from this side of the road. It would present an oblique angle, but for a sharpshooter that shouldn't be a problem.

As Nimrod reached the door, Devine emerged from the mercantile. Devine didn't look his way and Nimrod headed on to the next building with a determined stride.

To Nimrod's relief, the saloon-owner was standing at the door. He moved to block Nimrod's way.

'We're closed,' he said. 'You can drink your fill when the speeches are over.'

'I'm not interested in the speeches,' Nimrod said. 'I want to see your guest — the one who arrived last night, injured, desperate.'

The owner bit his lip while looking around to check nobody was close.

'Room five,' he whispered while moving past Nimrod down the boardwalk.

As Halloway was urging everyone to welcome Maddox, in a matter of moments the target would be on the podium and visible from the rooms above, so Nimrod wasted no time in slipping inside.

He took the stairs lightly while still hurrying. When he reached the corridor at the top he counted the doors and saw that room five would be the last room.

He edged along beside the opposite wall of the corridor, treading close to the wall to limit creaking. He stopped at a point opposite the last door.

For several seconds he listened, hearing no sounds coming from within the room. But he didn't have enough time to be cautious. So, despite the risk, he drew his gun and took two long paces. He kicked the door.

He had thought it unlikely that it would be unlocked, but to his surprise the door swung open. He ran in and dodged to the left. Sheridan was sitting in a chair beside the window with a rifle on his lap.

Nimrod trained his gun on him, but as Sheridan wasn't in a position either to return fire or to fire at Maddox through the window, he didn't shoot. Nimrod came to a halt in the corner of the room as Sheridan looked at him without surprise.

'The big man is making a lot of noise across the road,' Sheridan said, pointing through the window, 'but I'd reckoned that if anyone were to find me, it'd be you.'

'Quit the smart talk and put your rifle on the floor.'

Sheridan merely looked through the window, adopting a position where he could see the podium.

'Halloway has finished his speech. It was a good one. It's the only thing he does well. Maddox is droning on now, but he'll eventually come to the part Halloway has been waiting for. He'll state that Halloway is his closest friend, the man who'll be behind him in his quest to become the next governor.'

'And that's the moment when you'd planned to shoot him.' Nimrod raised his gun slightly and settled his stance, drawing Sheridan's attention back to his predicament. 'Except I won't let you.'

'What makes you think I plan to shoot Maddox Kingsley?'

Nimrod moved away from the corner. Through the window the crowd came into view below and, when he slipped around the bed to stand behind Sheridan, he could see the podium where both Maddox and Halloway were standing.

'Because you're sitting here with a rifle watching him.'

Sheridan leaned back and offered him a thin smile.

'I'm not watching Maddox Kingsley. I'm watching Mayor Halloway.'

'Halloway?' Nimrod murmured. 'You saying you're planning to kill the mayor?'

'Mayor Halloway is a festering thorn in Bigelow Town's hide. Except nobody knows about anything he's done in his quest for power. Cornelius does. He used to do his bidding, but no more.

Halloway must be stopped and who better than the man he worked so hard to hire?'

'What proof do you have?'

'None. Halloway is careful and even if Sheriff Thorndike had the guts and the brains to charge him, he'd hire the best lawyers and escape justice. That's why he has to be killed.'

Nimrod took a slow pace forward. 'You know I can't stand aside and let you shoot him.'

In response Sheridan calmly picked up the rifle and half-swung it towards the window.

'Devine wouldn't,' he said. 'He's a blunt instrument attached to a gun. But a Pinkerton detective must be able to see beyond simple matters of law.'

Sheridan had said the only thing that could give Nimrod doubts, but he still shook his head.

'I understand, but seeing is as far as I'll go. If there's corruption here, I'll root it out, but I'll do it the right way. I won't let you kill a man whom this town voted in as their mayor.'

'Then do what you think is right, as will I.'

Sheridan turned away. He swung the rifle to the side to aim through the window, carrying out his actions steadily to give Nimrod enough time to stop him if he chose to.

'Don't,' Nimrod said.

Sheridan felt his wounded side and shuffled to get himself into the right position.

Nimrod fired, making Sheridan jerk to one side.

Nimrod had shot him in the right arm; the wound was high and glancing, intending only to incapacitate him. Sheridan's shoulder slammed against the chair-back, then he slumped to one side, giving Nimrod an uninterrupted view of the road below.

The gunshot had broken through the hubbub, making people look around. On the podium Halloway and Maddox engaged in an animated conversation while two guards moved forward and gestured at them to go into the mayor's office.

Maddox delivered warding-off gestures, showing that he was refusing to leave. Then, inside the room above, Sheridan pushed himself upright and blocked Nimrod's view.

'Your aim was poor,' Sheridan said through gritted teeth.

'I gave you a second chance. If what you said has substance, you and Cornelius can give me the details: names, dates, events.'

Sheridan cast a quick look through the window. He shook his head sorrowfully.

'It'll never work. This is the only way.' He flashed a thin smile and snapped up the rifle. 'And I can use both hands.'

Despite his boast, with his multiple wounds he was unable to keep the rifle steady. But even a badly aimed gunshot at a crowded road was sure to hit someone. With a heavy heart Nimrod lowered his gun slightly and fired.

The second shot took Sheridan low

in the side close to the wound Devine had given him, making him cry out. He slid from his chair.

'Tell me quickly,' Nimrod said, standing over him. 'What's my best hope of defeating Mayor Halloway?'

'You've already done it,' Sheridan breathed, his voice fading fast. He turned up the corners of his mouth with a grim rictus that promised his death was imminent. 'I was the distraction.'

Nimrod knelt beside him, planning to ask him for more details before he breathed his last. But with a start he realized what Sheridan had meant.

'Cornelius Lee?' he said.

Sheridan couldn't reply; his eyes were glazing. Nimrod jumped to his feet. He looked down at the crowd below.

The people were parting as Marshal Devine waded into their midst to reach the podium. Nimrod ran his gaze to the politicians and saw what had attracted Devine's attention.

Cornelius Lee was moving through the crowd.

15

Nimrod hurtled down the stairs to the saloon room. He grabbed hold of the post at the bottom, swung himself round and ran on. He vaulted several fallen chairs in his haste before he burst out through the doors.

From the boardwalk he didn't have as good a view of the situation as he'd had from above, but he could see that a space was opening up before the podium.

A gunshot rang out from the crowd.

Mayor Halloway stumbled forward clutching his chest. Then he toppled over the rail at the front of the podium to lie with his arms dangling.

People cried out in alarm as they tried to spread out from the scene of the shooting, but they were met by the solid mass of the crowd filling the road. Those on the fringes ran away for a few paces and then turned to see what was happening, their actions only hindering the escape of those who were closer to the podium.

Nimrod rapidly found that he was one of the few people moving towards the mayor's office. But so many people were ahead of him that they blocked his view of events and he had to shove people aside to make headway.

Another gunshot rang out and then a sharp volley of gunfire blasted, adding to the general confusion.

Nimrod fought on. He dodged and wove until, with a stumble as he fell over a fallen man, he emerged into clear space.

Halloway was lying where he'd fallen. The two guards who had been close to him were lying on the ground, still and bloodied. Another of Maddox Kingsley's guards was checking on Halloway, but he was shaking his head and a fourth guard, while looking around, was shouting at him to leave Halloway alone.

Clearly they had yet to secure their prime responsibility's safety and, as they'd not been close to the podium when the gunfire had broken out, they were as unsure as Nimrod was about what exactly had happened.

When Nimrod hurried on towards the podium he couldn't see Maddox, neither could he see Cornelius. Only one man was moving with purpose: Devine was striding across the boardwalk to the mayor's office. He stopped to listen for several seconds before he kicked open the door and then darted in.

This unusual level of caution suggested that Cornelius had gone to ground inside, perhaps having taken Maddox hostage. With the other guards still struggling to make sense of the situation, Nimrod decided to trust Devine's judgment.

He ran to the door where he listened, but, hearing nothing happening inside, he entered, to find that Devine was at the bottom of the stairs peering up.

'What did you waste your time doing?' Devine muttered.

'I found Sheridan Cox.'

'Still a problem?'

'No.'

Devine grunted, the sound registering approval for the first time about something he'd done.

'That leaves Cornelius. He's kidnapped Maddox.'

Devine gestured at the stairs and stepped back a pace. Although Nimrod was sure he hadn't gained his respect, he went up the stairs first, with Devine at his heels. The door to the mayor's office was closed, the other doors were open.

Nimrod stepped along the side of the corridor. Devine strode down the centre, his footfalls heavy enough to be heard in the office.

As he was unsure where Cornelius would be, Nimrod stopped at the door to plan how he would get into the mayor's office quickly. But the moment he moved for the door, Devine clamped a hand on his shoulder.

'What you — ?'

Nimrod didn't get to complete his question before Devine launched him at the door. Unable to stop himself, Nimrod hammered into the wood.

At the last moment he raised his right arm to shield himself, but the door still flew open so quickly it almost broke free, and Nimrod could do nothing but stumble on for two uncertain paces; then he keeled over. He tried to turn his fall into a roll, but he failed and instead he slid along the floor on his side.

During his unplanned entrance he noticed two men standing beside the window, but he landed in a position where he couldn't see them. As he raised himself to confirm that the men were Cornelius and Maddox, Devine paced in after him.

'Back away from that worthless snake, Cornelius,' he roared.

'The situation is under control,' Maddox said, glaring at Devine with more apparent concern about the marshal's harsh words than the fact that Cornelius had a gun on him. 'We're just discussing what happened.'

Nimrod got to his feet just as, despite Maddox's comment, Cornelius swung Maddox round to place him between his own body and Devine.

'No talk,' Devine said. 'Release him.'

Maddox spread his hands. 'According to Cornelius, Mayor Halloway was secretly behind most of the trouble that's happened in Jackson County. Apparently, he'd planned to have me killed while Cornelius and his friends were working to extract money from him to support the mission. I believe him and I'm prepared to hear him out, after which he's agreed to lower his gun.'

Devine said nothing, but he raised his gun slightly, giving the impression that he was sighting Cornelius over Maddox's shoulder.

It was a risky act, such as Nimrod wouldn't attempt. Then again, he wasn't Devine.

'Ignore Devine's threat,' Nimrod said, taking a pace forward. 'I won't let him shoot you. I want to find a way out of this for all of us.'

'Don't believe you,' Cornelius called over Maddox's shoulder. He cast an angry glare at Nimrod. 'I trust Devine more than I trust a Pinkerton man.'

'You should trust your friend more,' Devine muttered. 'I'm saving the no-worth piece of scum who got his sorry hide elected.'

Maddox flashed a brief smile at Nimrod, acknowledging the irony of a situation where the man he wanted dead was trying to save his life. Then he shook his head.

'You won't. Today finally ended the childhood squabbles that filled our days at the mission and have done ever since. So I'll listen to Cornelius and you'll follow my orders, Devine.'

Nimrod nodded, seeing that Maddox had chosen his words carefully to give him a reason to confront Devine, but Nimrod had a better one.

'Devine, you used me to draw Cornelius's fire,' he said. He waited for Devine to look at him, but the marshal didn't look away from his target. 'I never thought you'd turn out to be a yellow-belly.'

He settled his stance as he waited for Devine to turn his ire on him, but Devine stood impassive and silent.

'That doesn't surprise me,' Maddox said. 'Cornelius told me about the Devil's Hump massacre. This mayhem must stop, Devine. Leave us to discuss what Cornelius knows about Mayor Halloway.'

Devine didn't move a muscle and, as long moments dragged on, Nimrod turned back to the hostage and captor. He took another pace towards them, which made Cornelius glance at him with his eyes still narrowed from anger after meeting the man who had double-crossed him.

That was all the distraction Devine needed.

A gunshot roared, the sound echoing in the room.

Blood flew from Cornelius's shoulder as he flinched away from Maddox who, in uncertainty over what had happened, doubled over. That only gave Devine a clearer target. He slammed more lead into Cornelius's chest, making him fall to the floor.

As Cornelius twitched and then stilled, Devine walked across the office to glare down at the body. He kicked Cornelius's side, but his form moved lifelessly.

'Nobody wants to listen to you,' he said. He splattered a long drool of spit on his forehead.

'You gun-toting fool,' Maddox said, standing upright to confront him. 'I aim to make this county safe for decent folk to live in, but I can't do that if you shoot up the people who want to help me.'

'He killed Mayor Halloway.'

'And he had good reason. Halloway was corrupt. He even used me in his twisted plans. That needed to be exposed.'

'Politicians make speeches,' Devine muttered with contempt, turning to the desk. 'Lawmen make the law.'

'You don't. You kill indiscriminately. My use of the law is the right one. I support the proper process of gathering evidence and confirming facts.'

Devine dragged open the bottom drawer of Halloway's desk and extracted a saddle-bag. He withdrew a handful of bills from the bag and then hurled the saddle-bag across the office to Nimrod's feet.

'Halloway's bounty,' he said waving the money at Maddox, 'and a bribe to the men he hired to kill you.'

'That evidence isn't enough,' Maddox said, although he lowered his tone presumably in surprise that Devine had been shrewd enough to gather proof of Halloway's activities. 'And worse, Cornelius would have given me the names of the others who helped Halloway.'

'Who needs names?' Devine glanced at his gun. 'You have me.'

Maddox looked at Nimrod and held his gaze for a moment, clearly ordering him to take on Devine, but Devine mistook his eye-flick and followed his gaze to the saddlebag and the money poking out of the top.

Devine snorted. He hefted the bills in his hand and paced up to Maddox, who stood his ground.

Devine sneered. Then he darted forward and grabbed Maddox's jaw.

'Get off me,' Maddox said, but Devine ignored him. He prised open his lips and then stuffed the bills in his mouth.

Maddox spluttered out several slips of paper, but that only encouraged Devine to cram more bills into his mouth until his lips were spread widely around a circle of paper. He stood back to admire his work.

'You like seeing a politician dining on money, Pinkerton man?' he asked.

'I reckon,' Nimrod said, 'that treating a man who could be the next governor with contempt is unacceptable.'

'He has nothing to offer.'

Devine turned away, leaving Maddox

to splutter and use his fingers to extract the bills. When he'd cleared enough space to breathe, he glared at Nimrod while pointing at Devine's back.

With a long sigh Nimrod turned to Devine at the same moment as Devine darted round to face him, making Nimrod gulp. Then he saw that Devine wasn't interested in him. He was looking past his head at the door.

A moment later footfalls sounded as several men hurried down the corridor. Then, in a strident voice Maddox cried out.

'I'm in here and so is Devine,' he shouted. He paused to spit out the last of the bills. 'Kill him. Kill them all!'

Nimrod swung round to face the open door while Devine hurried to the right to gain a different angle.

The pounding footfalls stopped, the last pattering sounds being on either side of the doorway. Nimrod reckoned that at least four of Maddox's guards had come down the corridor, but as they'd reached points of safety without showing themselves through the open doorway, he couldn't be sure of their number.

'Who else is in there?' one of the guards shouted.

'Just Nimrod Dunn,' Maddox shouted. 'He won't be no trouble.'

Nimrod looked for Maddox, but he had ducked down behind the desk and was now out of view. Then Nimrod did as Devine had done and paced sideways ensuring that when the guards came in, they would face trouble from different angles.

'The shooting you heard in here,' Nimrod said while still walking, 'was Cornelius Lee getting shot up. Nobody needs rescuing.'

'Don't listen to him,' Maddox shouted. 'Devine has gone loco and Nimrod is refusing to do his duty.'

A murmured comment sounded outside. Then two men hurried in.

One man went left and one man went right. They came in low and fast, but they both found themselves running towards drawn guns.

Two gunshots rang out as Devine and Nimrod dispatched them with fast and deadly gunshots. Devine's target stood up straight having been hit high in the chest, giving Devine an easy target for his second shot to the forehead, which felled him.

Nimrod's aim was hurried and less accurate. He hit his target low in the side. The man ran on, the pain making him struggle to raise his gun.

Nimrod tried to step aside, but the man ran into him. For a moment they made eye contact. Then Nimrod fired a second time, the shot flashing heat across his hand at point-blank range.

Another gunshot tore out behind him and, when the man's weight fell against him, Nimrod saw that the other two guards had come in.

The man who had approached Devine was already falling, but the second man ran towards him. His view of Nimrod being blocked by Nimrod's first assailant, he stilled his fire.

With only a moment to react Nimrod jerked his arm up to shoot him, but the man he'd already shot was still sliding away from him and his hand caught in his jacket.

While freeing himself, Nimrod side-stepped away. His motion gave his new assailant enough room to throw himself forward. He caught Nimrod around the shoulders and forced him backwards.

Nimrod back-stepped twice while, over his assailant's shoulder, he saw Devine charge out into the corridor, firing on the run. Then his opponent's relentless pressure made him tumble.

He went all his length and slid across the floor until he fetched up against the wall. The crown of his head slammed into the wall, stunning him.

His assailant took advantage of Nimrod's sudden weakness and jerked his gun up. Rapid gunfire out in the corridor helped to jar Nimrod's senses and, from the corner of his eye, he saw his opponent's gun swing towards his head.

With a reflex action he threw up a hand. Luckily, at the first attempt his hand closed around the man's wrist and, with his elbow planted to the floor, he had enough leverage to still the gun's motion.

The man strained, moving himself up Nimrod's body to plant a knee on his chest. Then, with the extra traction, he strained to move the gun in. Inch by inch the weapon moved towards Nimrod's head.

A gunshot roared, and then a second.

The man twitched as he glared down at him and for a moment Nimrod thought he'd fired before he reached his target. But then the pressure on his arm slackened and the man fell away to reveal Devine standing in the doorway.

The marshal took a long pace forward and slammed more lead into the attacker's lifeless body.

'Check the building, Pinkerton man,' he said, moving over to the other guards he'd dispatched earlier.

Nimrod shook himself, partially clearing his stunned senses, then he got to his feet. Still disoriented by the blow to the head, he hurried to the door. He listened, then slipped out into a corridor.

Two men lay sprawled at the top of the stairs, their backs holed. Nimrod went to the stairs, but he saw nobody down below.

He thought back to his meeting with Maddox Kingsley in the stage and mentally counted the number of guards who had accompanied him. He judged that the ones they'd dispatched here along with the men Cornelius had killed accounted for them all, along with several men he hadn't known worked for Maddox.

Feeling more optimistic, he checked the other rooms before he went up to a storeroom where he found only a comatose Gilchrist Wheaton. Then he returned to the mayor's office to find Devine standing by the desk with his gun aimed at the cowering Maddox Kingsley.

'Nobody threatens me and lives,' Devine said levelly.

'Don't shoot,' Maddox said, his voice shaking.

He looked up at Devine; then, on finding no comfort in his cold gaze he looked at Nimrod. But after Maddox's earlier order Nimrod returned only a slow shake of the head.

'Plead for your life, politician man,' Devine said.

Without hesitation Maddox rolled forward on to his knees and placed his hands together in an attitude of prayer.

'Please,' he said, 'I was wrong. I need lawmen like you to enforce justice.'

'Spill the rest.'

'That's all I can say.'

Maddox again flicked his gaze to Nimrod, this time with less hope than before. Nimrod hefted the gun in his hand to draw Maddox's attention to the fact that he was keeping it lowered and that he would complete his mission only in a way of his choosing.

'Devine,' he said, 'we'll tell everyone what Maddox ordered his guards to do. Don't shoot an unarmed man.'

'You're right, Pinkerton man,' Devine said. 'A lead dinner is too good for him.'

Devine slapped a heavy hand on Maddox's jacket and dragged him to his feet. He drew him up on to tiptoe so that the two men could look at each other eye to eye.

Devine looked deep into the other man's eyes. Whatever he saw there made him sneer.

'Tell me what you want,' Maddox said with a loud gulp, 'and you can have it.'

'Wrong offer,' Devine said. With an angry oath, he hurled him aside.

Maddox hit the centre of the windowpane head first. In a shower of glass he went tumbling from view. A few moments later a crash sounded.

Devine went to the window to look down. He nodded approvingly and then beckoned Nimrod to join him.

Still shocked by Devine's action, Nimrod hurried to the window. Maddox had landed on the podium near to Halloway's body. He'd broken through the boards to deposit them both unceremoniously on the ground.

The people who had dispersed when the shooting started were emerging from hiding to drift closer, craning their necks with a mixture of shock and, Nimrod reckoned, relief.

'This is what you do, isn't it?' Nimrod said. 'You don't investigate, or worry about the rights and wrongs, or try to work out who is guilty and who is innocent. It's whoever threatens you dies.'

'Took you a while, Pinkerton man,' Devine said, moving away from the window, 'but you got there in the end.'

Devine considered the dollars that were spilling out of Halloway's saddlebag. He gathered up a handful and stuffed them in a pocket before he made for the door.

'So now that you've killed the outlaws,' Nimrod shouted after him, 'killed everyone who helped them, killed the politicians, and killed the politicians' guards, that means your mission is over.'

Devine stopped in the doorway to consider him.

'It's never over. There's always scum to wipe out.'

'There is.' Nimrod raised both arms until he'd aimed his cocked gun at Devine's chest. He held the weapon steady, with his left hand holding his right wrist. 'So now you can deal with the threat from me.'

Devine looked at the gun. Then he moved his gaze up to meet Nimrod's eyes.

A smile appeared. Then Devine laughed; a long, deep belly laugh, his mirth shaking his beard. When Nimrod blinked hard in surprise at his reaction, he laughed all the harder.

Nimrod tried to tighten his trigger finger, but Devine's lack of concern made a tremor start up in his biceps and it was all he could do to keep the gun aimed in the general direction of the doorway.

He knew he was leaving himself open to be shot in retaliation, but instead, Devine leaned to the side to spit on the face of one of the dead guards. Then he turned and left the office, leaving Nimrod with his gun aimed at an empty doorway.

As Devine clumped down the stairs he whistled a merry tune.

16

'I've heard,' Weddell Johnson said, leaning over Nimrod's shoulder, 'that you want to join us.'

'Sure,' Nimrod said. He drank the last dregs of his whiskey in a long gulp and then placed the glass on the bar. He turned to consider Weddell along with his three companions.

The information he'd received for his first mission after leaving Bigelow Town was that these four men were bank raiders. They'd been rendered ineffective recently when Conrad Dagwood, their safe breaker, had been killed.

Nimrod's mission was to become Conrad's replacement.

Weddell spread his hands and gestured around the sparsely populated saloon.

'Then tell us more,' he said with a smile. 'We're amongst friends here.'

Nimrod sneered. 'I can see why Conrad Dagwood got shot to pieces. Senseless prattle gets men killed.'

Two men moved in with anger in their eyes, but Weddell raised an arm, holding them back.

'You interested or not?'

'I'm interested, but not here.'

Nimrod gestured to the stairs, but he wasn't surprised when Weddell indicated the door instead.

With Weddell leading and the other three men glaring at him after his insult, they went outside. At a steady pace they walked down the main road in Prudence to the back of the stables where, in the low moonlight, they surrounded him.

'Barney said you're the best,' Weddell said.

The saloon-owner Barney Root would say anything for the right price, but Nimrod nodded.

'Hear about the bank raid in Liberty?'

Weddell raised his eyebrows while the

others murmured in interest for the first time.

'You did that?'

'Nope. I was planning to, but someone else got to the bank first.'

They all stared at him in bemusement, but when Nimrod smiled, they caught on and snorted laughs.

'Barney also said you're a joker. Riding with you should be interesting.'

'So where are we going?'

'Redemption City.'

'A tough bank,' Nimrod said, rubbing his jaw. 'It'll take time.'

'We're patient. It might take months, but for a nut that sweet, it'll be worth the wait.'

'I used to be patient. These days I prefer a direct approach.'

'What's that?' Weddell asked, leaning forward, as did the other three men.

Nimrod stepped backwards for a pace and craned his neck as he looked around, as if checking they were alone. The men followed his gaze, but his movement had been designed to distract them from seeing him draw his gun.

With a quick motion, he hammered lead into Weddell's guts. Then he splayed gunfire to the right, taking out the nearest two men.

Only the last man had enough time to draw his gun, but before he could fire Nimrod barged into him and knocked him to his knees. A hastily aimed shot to the chest dispatched him.

He confirmed the men were dead. Then he paced over the bodies and made his way back to the road. He didn't holster his gun.

From the safety of the shadows people stared at him, torn between avoiding and confronting a man who was coming from the place where gunfire had sounded. He ignored them and strode with determined steps to the law office.

'Mission complete,' he said when he opened the door.

'Already?' Sheriff Simmons said, raising his eyebrows in surprise. 'You only arrived an hour ago.'

Nimrod came inside and sat on the sheriff's vacant chair. He considered whether he should provide the details, but he decided not to waste his time.

Instead, he slapped his feet on the sheriff's desk and leaned back in his chair. When he saw the awe and perhaps even a hint of fear in the lawman's eyes, he felt so elated that he whistled a contented tune.

THE END

Other titles in the
Linford Western Library:

NINE DEAD MEN

Walter L. Bryant

Ten years after his life is saved, Jason drifts into Inspiration. He believes fate has given him an opportunity to repay the debt when he hears of the leader of an outlaw gang, Adam One-ear. But his determination to meet Adam is complicated by the intervention of a sheriff who wants to kill the outlaw, a young man seeking revenge for an old injustice, and the abduction of the rancher's daughter. When Jason, the sheriff and Adam meet for the final time, nine men have already died . . .

DOUBLE CROSS TRAIL DRIVE

Chet Cunningham

The journey begins as an ordinary trail drive from Texas to the railroad in Kansas — but soon turns deadly as bullets fly and rustlers try to steal the whole herd of steer . . . Back at the ranch in Texas, the violence continues, as the ranch owner seems to have become a sitting target. Whoever is out to ruin the ranch and kill the owner must be discovered, especially as the final deadly cattle stampede threatens to settle the matter once and for all . . .

DUEL OF SHADOWS

Billy Hall

Eli Lowenstein has been murdered, and Sam Murray wasn't the man who took his life. But when the accusers threaten to look in his saddle-bags, he remembers the strange noises he heard that night, and the talk of the planted evide[illegible] demned Ephraim [illegible] lynching. He's su[illegible] anything he'll sw[illegible] a rope, just like [illegible] there's no way S[illegible] to sit back and [illegible] noose over his he[illegible]